She moved to pass him, but he didn't immediately step out of the way, bringing them even closer together.

His gaze held hers when he reached up unexpectedly to brush the ends of her angled bob, his fingertips just brushing her cheek. "Your hair is different," he murmured. "Shorter and darker."

Self-conscious, she shrugged. "I stopped bleaching it. And it's easier to wear it shorter with my busy schedule now."

"It looks good."

Uncertain how to take the compliment, she merely said, "Thank you."

He continued to search her face, as if noting every slight difference. "More than just your hair has changed."

"That's hardly surprising," she answered with forced lightness. "I was just a kid when we met, now I'm a thirty-year-old mother of school-age twins. Of course I've changed."

"You were a pretty girl," he replied. "You're a beautiful woman."

Her eyes closed for just a moment, her cheeks going warm. His simple statement had rocked her to her toes.

Dear Reader,

Friends who become lovers has always been one of my favorite romance themes—mostly because I think friendship is an important basis for any lasting relationship. My husband, John, and I have been best friends and partners for more than thirty years, and that foundation has sustained us through both the good times and the inevitable challenges life has thrown our way.

In *His Best Friend's Wife,* I added a few extra complications. The tangled emotions Evan and Renae have about her late husband—his best friend—her six-year-old twins, and her very present, very meddling and very antagonistic-toward-Evan mother-in-law, Lucy. Not only does Evan have to woo Renae, he has to somehow convince Lucy to give him a chance in the tightly knit family unit they've formed. The odds are stacked against him, but he believes it's worth the effort, if he can only persuade Renae....

I hope you enjoy this story I had so much pleasure writing for you. Visit me at my blog site, ginawilkins.com, or my Facebook page for news about upcoming Harlequin releases!

Gina Wilkins

HIS
BEST FRIEND'S
WIFE

GINA WILKINS

HARLEQUIN®
entertain, enrich, inspire™

Recycling programs
for this product may
not exist in your area.

ISBN-13: 978-0-373-65688-2

HIS BEST FRIEND'S WIFE

Copyright © 2012 by Gina Wilkins

GINA WILKINS

is a bestselling and award-winning author who has written more than seventy novels for Harlequin Books. She credits her successful career in romance to her long, happy marriage and her three "extraordinary" children.

A lifelong resident of central Arkansas, Ms. Wilkins sold her first book to Harlequin in 1987 and has been writing full-time since. She has appeared on the Waldenbooks, B. Dalton and *USA TODAY* bestseller lists. She is a three-time recipient of a Maggie Award for Excellence, sponsored by Georgia Romance Writers, and has won several awards from the reviewers of *RT Book Reviews*.

For my husband and best friend, John

Chapter One

"I have always been delighted at the prospect of
a new day, a fresh try, one more start, with perhaps a bit of magic waiting somewhere behind
the morning…"

—Joseph Priestley

"Excuse me? Is this where I sign in for my appointment with Dr. Sternberg?"

Renae Sanchez picked up a stack of clipboards for
the sign-in counter of the optometrists' office where she
worked as office manager. Pasting a professional smile
on her face, she turned to greet the man who'd spoken
from the other side of the open reception window.

The clipboards hit the floor with a crash that made
several people in the waiting room jump in their seats.
Embarrassed, Renae gave them an apologetic look

before gathering the scattered clipboards and attempting to collect her composure. Only then did she approach the counter—and the man from her past who waited there.

Except for the slight hint of gray at the temples of his conservatively cut, coffee-colored hair, Evan Daugherty looked much the same as he had the last time she had seen him almost seven years ago, as a pallbearer at her late husband's funeral.

In his early thirties, Evan's face was slightly more tanned now from years of working outdoors, and the little squint lines that had developed at the corners of his dark eyes only added to the appeal of his ruggedly attractive features. He'd had tears in those dark brown eyes the last time she'd seen him. He smiled now— though his smile froze when she faced him fully.

She had identified him at first glance, but it seemed to have taken him a heartbeat longer to make the connection. Had she changed so much in the past seven years? She had been twenty-three, six months pregnant with twins and in a haze of shock and grief when they last parted. Seeing him now sent those long-banked feelings flooding through her again—in addition to other complex reactions to Evan himself.

Working especially hard to ignore the latter emotions, she kept her expression carefully schooled when she set the clipboards on the counter. "Hello, Evan."

Tactfully, he merely glanced at the clipboards, declining to comment on her clumsy response to the sight of him. "Renae. This is a surprise."

"For me, too," she agreed. "I didn't see your name on the appointment list."

She wasn't usually the one who checked in clients,

but as her luck would have it, Lisa was at lunch and Cathy was busy with a phone call.

"You're looking well." Though Evan spoke easily, Renae sensed that he felt as awkward as she did about this unexpected reunion.

Or was she merely projecting? Was she the only one suddenly remembering a forbidden kiss on a tumultuous night that had sporadically haunted her dreams— and sometimes her unguarded waking moments—for almost a decade?

All too aware that they were being idly watched by the waiting clients whose attention had been drawn by the crashing clipboards, she kept her tone as politely professional as she could, considering the turmoil inside her. "What can I do for you, Evan?"

"Oh. Right. I have an appointment with Dr. Sternberg. I just need to give you my insurance information."

He offered her an insurance card and she was pleased—and somewhat surprised—to note that her hand was steady as she took it from him and handed him a clipboard in return. "I'll make a copy of this for your file. If you'll have a seat and fill out this new-patient form, Dr. Sternberg will be with you shortly."

He hesitated before turning away, looking as though he found their brief, strictly business exchange unsatisfying. "How are the twins?"

"They're well, thank you. Growing like weeds." She almost winced at hearing the overused cliché from her own lips, but it was the best she could do just then.

"Excuse me, Renae, you have a call on line three."

She turned gratefully in response to the welcome interruption. "Thank you, Cathy. Will you make a copy of Mr. Daugherty's insurance information, please?"

"Of course."

With a coolly civil nod to Evan, Renae took the phone call. She handled the business issue swiftly, then murmured an excuse to Cathy and escaped to the employees' restroom. Once there, she would have splashed cold water on her face, but she didn't want to wash off the makeup she'd barely had time to apply earlier after dressing hastily for work in a simple lavender sweater and gray pants. Instead, she leaned against the wall and closed her eyes, trying to collect her thoughts.

Barely fifteen minutes ago, she had asked aloud, "Could anything else go wrong today?" Having Evan Daugherty walk into her place of business out of the blue must be her punishment for tempting fate.

This October Tuesday morning had been hectic from the moment her alarm blasted her out of bed at 6:00 a.m. The twins dashed around the house frantically searching for shoes and backpacks, complaining about the healthy lunches she packed for them, suddenly remembering they were supposed to take a favorite stuffed animal because Tuesday was "animal kingdom day" in first grade. That led to lengthy debates about the toys to choose, which necessitated sharp words from Renae to keep them from being late, which, in turn, caused Renae's live-in mother-in-law, Lucy, to give Renae wounded looks for snapping at her precious grandchildren.

Lucy knew better than to openly challenge Renae's authority.

By the time the twins were safely delivered to school and Renae arrived at work, the usual chaos there was almost a welcome relief.

As the office manager for two young optometrists,

Renae performed many duties along with the two office workers she supervised, Cathy and Lisa. She answered phones, handled insurance claims, kept records for the accountant, checked in patients and scheduled appointments when necessary—anything she had to do to keep the office running with the efficiency she took such pride in. Two optometry assistants worked with Ann Boshears and Gary Sternberg, the married couple who'd moved to North Little Rock, Arkansas, a year earlier to set up their practice. They had hired Renae after she'd seen their ad in the newspaper—a nice promotion from the clerical position she'd held before in another medical office.

Renae had worked well from the start with Ann and Gary, and liked all her coworkers to varying degrees. As much as she loved her children and her mother-in-law, it was nice having a life away from home. She needed this outside interaction with other people, needed to feel that she was a competent, intelligent, self-sufficient woman in addition to being a mom and a daughter.

Yet all it had taken was an unexpected encounter with Evan Daugherty to undo her hard-earned progress and send her spinning back into the emotional mess she'd been when he had first met her almost ten years ago. Angry with herself, she drew a deep, bracing breath and opened her eyes, glaring at her reflection in the mirror. She thought she'd done a decent job of hiding her reactions from Evan and any onlookers, not counting that one paralyzed moment when the clipboards had tumbled to the floor. Now it was time to pull herself together and get back to work.

It had probably been inevitable that she would run into Evan again sometime. After all, they lived in adjacent cities in Central Arkansas, and worked in the same metropolitan area surrounding the capital city of Little Rock. Because he'd stayed in touch once a year through Christmas cards with formal little notes written inside, she knew he'd moved back to the area three years ago after a stint in the army. A few months later, he had started a landscape design business with Tate Price, an old friend who had also known her late husband, Jason.

Probably the only reason their paths hadn't crossed before now was because they had both avoided chance encounters as much as possible. It had been stressful enough hearing from him through the mail a few times lately in regard to the scholarship he and Tate had recently established in her husband's memory.

Feeling her responsibilities calling her, she squared her shoulders, lifted her chin and left the restroom, glad to see that Evan was no longer in the waiting room. He must be in with Dr. Sternberg. She hoped Lisa would get back from lunch so Renae could leave before he came out again. As cowardly as it made her feel, she would just as soon avoid another awkwardly public exchange with him today.

No such luck. Renae hadn't yet had a chance to escape when Evan reappeared just as she delivered a file to Cathy, putting them both at the payment window at the same time.

"I'm just leaving for lunch. Cathy will take your payment," she said, nodding pleasantly to him when he looked at her as though expecting her to say something. "It was good to see you again, Evan."

Cordial and poised. Exactly the tone she'd hoped to achieve, she applauded herself.

"Good to see you, too, Renae." He glanced at her

coworkers before saying tentatively, "Actually, I've been wanting to contact you about the scholarship program. Maybe we could have a bite together and discuss it?"

Sitting near enough to overhear, Cathy cleared her throat noisily and gave Renae a look that made it clear she thought she should accept Evan's offer. No surprise—Cathy was always trying to fix her up with someone, and she would no doubt view Evan as an attractive, charming and intriguing possibility. Which, of course, he would be, had it not been for the convoluted history between them.

"I'm sorry, Evan, I have an appointment," she lied without compunction, unable to face the thought of sitting across a little table from him without more preparation. But because she was interested in hearing about the scholarship progress, she scribbled her number and handed it to him. "Call any evening after work and I'd be happy to discuss the scholarship with you."

She could handle talking with Evan on the phone, she assured herself. Maybe the painful emotions wouldn't assail her so forcefully if she weren't looking at him while they talked. Maybe she would be less likely to embarrass herself with her awkward reactions to him, the way she had today.

If he was disappointed that she'd declined his lunch invitation, it didn't show on his face when he folded the paper and tucked it into the pocket of the navy twill shirt he wore with neatly pressed khakis. "I'll be in contact."

She nodded, ignored Cathy's frown of disapproval and turned to make a determinedly dignified—if still hasty—escape.

She drove several blocks away, pulled into the parking lot of a fast-food restaurant and buried her face in her hands, only then letting the memories overwhelm her.

Six hours later, Evan sat in his living room, staring glumly out at the Little Rock skyline across the Arkansas River from his fifth-floor apartment. He lived on the North Little Rock side of the river, driving across the Broadway Bridge every morning to the office of Price-Daugherty Landscape Design, the company he owned with his longtime friend, Tate Price. He'd chosen this place specifically for this view. He had spent too many evenings since admiring it alone.

He'd known since he'd moved back to this area that Renae Ingle Sanchez lived on the other side of that river. He had made no effort to seek her out since his return, communicating with her only by regular mail—a Christmas card every year for the past six years, and more recently information about the scholarship he and his business partner had established in her late husband's honor. He'd always wondered when they would run into each other again, figuring it would have to happen sometime, but he certainly hadn't been prepared to do so today.

Judging by the way those clipboards had hit the floor at her feet, she hadn't been prepared, either. Or had that moment of clumsiness had nothing to do with her seeing him standing there?

How many times had he thought about calling her, trying to see her? Too many to count. Yet something always held him back. Something that felt suspiciously like guilt. And maybe uncertainty about how she would react to hearing from him. After all, Renae's mother-in-law had once openly blamed Evan for Jason's death. While Renae hadn't echoed the words, she hadn't spoken out in Evan's defense, either.

He'd wondered if that was because she hadn't wanted to further upset her mother-in-law—or if it was because she agreed, even subconsciously, that Evan bore some responsibility for the tragedy. He had tried since to convince himself that while her silence might have hurt his feelings a little, he understood that she'd been in a bad place emotionally and hadn't been thinking clearly. He couldn't be angry with her any more than he could with Jason's inconsolable mother.

There were other emotions tangled up in his memories of Renae, but he didn't want to dwell on them too deeply at the moment. He confined himself to thinking about their encounter today.

She had changed. At first, he hadn't even been certain the woman behind the reception desk really was Renae. But when she'd looked at him straight on and he'd seen her eyes, there had been no doubt.

Though she had been polite enough, he couldn't say she had been particularly warm in greeting him. He supposed that made sense; there was too much history between them for a chance encounter to be easy and breezy. Not to mention that their surprise reunion was rather public. He hadn't been able to read her expression well enough to tell whether seeing him was merely awkward for her or genuinely painful.

He had found her attractive in her early twenties— too much so since she'd been the girlfriend and then the wife of one of his best friends—but she was even prettier at the dawn of her thirties. He remembered her hair being long and tousled, bleached to near white. Now she wore it in a sleek, darker blond bob that nicely framed her oval face. Her eyes looked larger and softer without the black eyeliner she'd favored back then, but they were still the vivid blue he remembered so clearly. Of average height, she was still slim. Maybe she'd gained a few pounds, but the soft curves looked good on her. Womanly, as opposed to girlish.

He knew she hadn't remarried, but he didn't know if she was seeing anyone. Did a working, single mom of six-and-a-half-year-old twins even have time to go out? Not that it was any of his business. She had made that clear enough at Jason's funeral, when she and Jason's mother had walked away from him without a backward glance.

It hadn't been the first time he and Renae had parted painfully. Two years earlier, while she was still dating Jason, they had shared one illicit kiss, spurred by forbidden infatuation and a few too many drinks. Though they had never crossed that line again, the attraction between them that night had been strong. Ill-advised, but mutual.

Did she ever wonder, as he did occasionally, what might have happened had he handled that episode differently?

Shaking his head in irritation, he pushed himself out of his chair and his memories. He had things to do tonight. He would call Renae, but when he did, it would be strictly about scholarship business. The past was just that—over and done. They had new lives now, new responsibilities. It was far too late for what-might-have-beens.

He'd have to remind himself of that every time those

old memories escaped the deep hole where he'd buried them years ago, until he finally convinced himself.

"Mom, Daniel's feeding Boomer from the table again."

"Am not!" Daniel set both hands hastily on the table, an exaggeratedly innocent look on his face.

Renae glanced at the small brown-and-white dog happily chewing something beneath her son's chair. "Don't fib, Daniel. And don't feed the dog from the table or I'm going to have to put him in the backyard when we eat."

Daniel sighed gustily, his dark hair falling over his forehead. Renae made a mental note to take him for a haircut Saturday. She would have had Lucy take him one day after school, but Lucy always insisted the barber cut Daniel's hair shorter than he liked now that he was in first grade. Renae figured some battles just weren't worth the trouble. Daniel was old enough to start expressing his preferences in clothing and hairstyle—within the limits Renae set, of course.

"Hunter got in trouble in school again today," Leslie said, indulging in her favorite pastime of gossiping about her classmates over dinner. "He wouldn't stop playing with his crayons when it was time for math lessons. Ms. Rice took his crayons away and he was mad."

"Hunter should listen to the teacher," Lucy said with a disapproving shake of her salt-and-pepper head. "I hope you two are behaving in your classes."

"Yes, ma'am," they chorused dutifully.

It had been at Renae's request that her children had been assigned to separate classes. They got along very well for the most part, for which she was grateful, but she thought it was good for them to form relationships as individuals and not just as "the twins."

"You aren't eating much this evening," Lucy commented, eyeing Renae's plate with a frown. Short, plump and matronly, widowed for almost two decades, Lucy dressed and often acted older than her fifty-nine years, resisting any attempts to modernize what Renae thought of as her housewife-y wardrobe, or to add any new activities to her life. She was content to keep house for her daughter-in-law and grandchildren, and attend the many church activities that kept her occupied while the kids were in school. "Aren't you feeling well? Do you not like the food?"

"The food is excellent, as always, Lucy," Renae answered patiently, taking a bite of the beef carnitas just to prove her point. Washing it down with a sip of peach-flavored iced tea, she then explained, "I had a late lunch today, so I'm not overly hungry tonight."

Lucy's eyebrows rose. "I thought you just took a turkey sandwich and a few carrot sticks for lunch. I figured you would be hungry tonight."

Lucy hadn't actually prepared the sandwich, because Renae insisted on making lunches for herself and the twins. It was one of the little things she did to make herself feel that she was pulling her weight around the house, despite Lucy taking the bulk of the cleaning and cooking. Still, Lucy kept an eye on what went out of "her" kitchen in brown bags and decorated lunch boxes.

Renae was reluctant to admit she'd left her turkey sandwich in the office fridge when she'd bolted after seeing Evan. She hadn't mentioned that encounter to Lucy yet, though she supposed she should. Maybe she would wait until the twins were in bed, and then try to find a way to break the news without unduly upsetting her mother-in-law, who still bristled whenever Evan's name came up after all these years.

Daniel squirmed restlessly in his seat, making Boomer wag his tail frantically in anticipation of fun. "I'm done with my dinner—may I go play now?"

"We have dessert," his grandmother reminded him, momentarily distracted from Renae's lack of appetite. "Fruit tarts."

Looking torn, Daniel glanced from his waiting pup toward the kitchen. "Can I have dessert later? I'm full."

"Go play for an hour, then you can have dessert after your bath," Renae agreed. "Leslie, do you want yours now or later?"

"Later," Leslie decided. "We're going to teach Boomer how to fetch."

"Good luck with that," Lucy said with a laugh and a shake of her head as the twins carried their plates and silverware carefully to the kitchen, accompanied by the eager dog. They would leave the plates on the counter by the sink for now, but when they were a little older, Renae would teach them to rinse and stack them in the dishwasher. She thought it important that both her children perform daily chores, so that everyone in the household made a contribution to its smooth functioning.

With her usual tenacity, Lucy returned her attention to Renae. "Are you not feeling well? Something seems to be off with you this evening."

Since the children were out of the room, Renae figured she might as well get this behind them. "There's something I need to tell you. A new patient came to the clinic today. Turns out it was someone we know."

"Oh?" Lucy stacked her fork and knife on her empty plate and laid her napkin on the table beside it. "Who was it?"

"Evan Daugherty."

She could almost feel the chill that settled over the room. Lucy froze in her chair, her eyes blackening to polished ebony. "Evan Daugherty showed up at your office today?"

"Yes. He had an appointment with Dr. Sternberg."

Every muscle in Lucy's body seemed to have gone stiff. "Why is he coming around you now? What does he want?"

"Lucy, his visit had nothing to do with me. He didn't even know I work for Dr. Sternberg."

The sharp sound she made clearly expressed Lucy's skepticism. "Did he try to talk to you?"

"We exchanged greetings. He asked about the twins."

"Their welfare is none of his business."

"He was merely being polite. People were watching."

"Is he coming back?"

"I don't know. If he made another appointment, it wasn't through me."

Lucy shook her head. "I hope he stays away. That man is bad news."

Renae moistened her lips with a sip of tea and braced herself for the reaction to her next admission. "I gave him my phone number. He's going to call sometime to discuss the scholarship he and Tate started in Jason's memory."

Predictably, Lucy scowled in disapproval. "You gave him your number? He must have pressured you into that. He's very good at talking people into things."

"He did not pressure me. He said he wanted to talk

with me about the scholarship and I gave him the number because I think it's a worthy cause. Simple as that."

Even the mention of the scholarship founded in her late son's honor didn't soften Lucy's expression. "Don't get mixed up with him, Renae. Evan Daugherty brings trouble. He was always getting my Jason into scrapes when they were boys and then he talked him into going out on those motorcycles when Jason should have been home with you getting ready for his babies."

There was a distinct quiver in her voice when she finished. Lucy held Evan responsible for Jason having the motorcycle in the first place. Evan had bought a used bike during his first year of college for commuting to classes, and Jason had subsequently decided he wanted one, too. Because Evan had helped Jason find a good deal, Lucy had always insisted that Evan had all but coerced her son into buying a dangerous motorbike.

Renae didn't have the heart to remind Lucy that Jason had been the one who had stubbornly insisted on going on that last ride, even though he had promised Renae he'd help her work on the nursery that weekend. Jason had argued with her, saying he wouldn't have many chances to get away once the kids arrived, and Renae had capitulated—as she so often had with Jason. Neither of them could have known, of course, that he would never return. That his life would end that afternoon beneath the wheels of a car that had sped through a stop sign without even slowing down.

Renae had been grateful ever since that she and Jason had parted with a kiss, despite the earlier quarrel, instead of hard words.

"This scholarship is important to me, Lucy," she said, trying to make her tone both firm and gentle at the same time. "The Jason Sanchez Memorial Scholarship will help young men go to college who might not have gone otherwise, and you know that would mean a lot to Jason."

At the time of his death, Jason had been a high school history teacher. Having already obtained his master's degree in history, he was just starting to work toward a doctorate degree, with the ultimate goal of teaching at a college level. A scholarship for at-risk young men was the perfect way to honor his memory, and despite her complex emotions concerning Evan Daugherty, Renae had been gratified to hear that one college freshman had already benefited from the effort.

"It was very generous of Evan and Tate to start this scholarship, and I'd like to be informed occasionally of its progress," she reiterated. "That doesn't mean I'll be getting mixed up with either of them."

"They're both trouble," Lucy repeated in an unhappy mutter. "Especially Evan."

Renae couldn't necessarily disagree with that, though her own reasons for thinking of Evan as trouble were distinctly different from Lucy's.

"I'll keep your warnings in mind." She stood and started gathering dirty dishes and glassware. There was no need to continue this conversation now. Lucy was in no mood to concede that Evan had any good intentions, and Renae was committed to supporting the scholarship effort in whatever way she could. Even if that meant crossing paths—or at least phone calls—occasionally with Evan, a prospect that made her pulse rate flutter erratically and annoyingly as she helped her mother-in-law clear away the remains of their dinner.

* * *

Evan called Thursday evening. Winding down from a day of school followed by Tae Kwon Do lessons, the twins, already bathed and in pajamas, sprawled on the floor watching their allotted hour of television. Lucy knitted on the couch while Renae read in her favorite easy chair. It was a rare quiet hour in the usually bustling household and the summons from Renae's cell phone was an intrusion despite the musical ringtone.

As if suspecting the identity of the caller, Lucy frowned. "Who is calling at this hour?"

Glancing at the ID screen, Renae swallowed. "I'll take it in another room. Kids, start getting ready for bed as soon as that program is over."

Without taking their attention from the television, they nodded. Renae lifted the phone to her ear as she left the room, avoiding her mother-in-law's disapproving stare. "Hello?"

Though she'd seen his name on the screen, Renae's stomach still tightened when she heard the deep voice in her ear. "Hi, Renae. I hope this isn't a bad time to call?"

She stepped into her tidy bedroom and closed the door. "No, it's fine."

"I mentioned to Tate that I saw you Tuesday. He said to tell you hello."

"Tell him hello back for me," she said lightly, sitting on the edge of her still-made bed.

"I will. So, anyway, he and I talked about the scholarship and we think we need to have a formal-ish meeting about it. You know, to get some guidelines in writing and figure out how to promote it and start seeking applications. We've been pretty haphazard about it so far, choosing Tate's new brother-in-law for the first recipient sort of impulsively—anyway, we want to do this correctly from now on. And we both wondered if you would like to be involved."

She followed his somewhat disjointed remarks with a baffled frown. "Involved in what way?"

"You know," he said, "working with us to outline the qualifications. Maybe read through applications and help us make our selections. That sort of thing. We've never administered a scholarship before, so this is all new to us."

"I don't have any experience with that, either," she said. And yet she found herself strongly tempted by his offer. As wary as she was about spending time with Evan, considering all the potential complications, she would hate for the scholarship to fall by the wayside because of a lack of effort on her part. "What can I do to help?"

"Tate suggested we could have a planning meeting right after work one evening, maybe over an early dinner. I know your evenings must be busy, with the kids and all, but would it be possible for you to join us one day next week?"

An after-work meeting with both Tate and Evan at a restaurant sounded innocuous enough—as much as possible, anyway. And a public venue would make the reunion even less awkward. "I'll be free next Wednesday evening after six. If that time is open for you and Tate, I could meet with you then."

"We'll make sure it's open. How does six next Wednesday sound for our first official meeting?"

It sounded soon. But she kept her nerves out of her voice when she said briskly, "Yes, that will be fine. Where shall we meet?"

"All the paperwork and stuff is at my place. We figured we could spread it all out there and discuss it without interruption. I can provide food. My apartment's not far from your office, so it should be convenient for you."

"At, uh, your place?"

"If that's agreeable for you?"

It was hardly the public restaurant she'd had in mind. Had he said all along the meeting would be at his home, she might have made an excuse not to go—but because her hesitation made her feel cowardly, she refused to change her answer now. "Yes, that will be fine."

"Would you like one of us to pick you up?" he offered.

"No, I'll drive. I'll just need the address."

She scribbled the address he gave her on a message pad she kept on her nightstand. She recognized the name of his apartment building, an upscale place only a few blocks from the eye clinic. She drove past it twice every weekday, but she'd no idea Evan lived there.

"You have my number if anything comes up in the meantime," Evan reminded her.

His number would show on the list of received calls on her phone. She would store it in her phone's contact list, just in case. "Yes, I have it."

"Good." His purported reason for the call out of the way, he moved to a more personal topic. "How have you been, Renae?"

"I'm well, thank you. And you?"

"Yeah, I'm good." Was that an undertone of dissatisfaction in his voice? Perhaps in response to her insistence on remaining businesslike, despite his own change in tone?

After a brief hesitation, Evan said, "Renae—this

scholarship. I just want you to know it means a lot to Tate and to me. I know we've been a little disorganized about it so far, but that doesn't mean we don't take it seriously. It's something we've talked about doing since we started our business. We hope Jason would approve."

She couldn't stay quite so brusque in response to his very obvious sincerity. Her voice sounded a bit softer to her own ears when she murmured, "I know it would please him very much that you and Tate have chosen to honor him this way."

"Thanks." He cleared his throat. "So I'll, uh, we'll see you Wednesday?"

"Yes. Wednesday."

Disconnecting the call, she sat for a few minutes longer in the silence of her sage-and-plum bedroom. A few photos were clustered on the cherry dresser that matched her bed and nightstand, furniture she'd purchased a year ago after starting her new job. She didn't glance at the frames that held pictures of her children and her late husband, but she was suddenly, acutely aware of them.

The meeting she and Evan had arranged was all about the scholarship, she reminded herself. There was no other reason for her to go to Evan's home, or to see him or Tate again. Lucy would probably accuse Evan of using the powers of persuasion she was sure he possessed to talk Renae into this meeting, but he'd done nothing more than offer her a chance to be involved with the program, and she had chosen to accept.

Maybe she wouldn't mention the meeting to Lucy just yet. It would only upset her unnecessarily. Once the scholarship was better established, Lucy would probably be more accepting of Renae's contact with Jason's former friends, especially since it would be clear that it was about honoring Jason's memory.

Having lost her biological mother when she was very young, Renae adored her mother-in-law, who had filled that gaping void with love and nurturing and stability. Renae would do nothing willingly to jeopardize that close relationship.

As confident as she had been that she'd made the right decision in choosing to attend the scholarship meeting, Renae still had second—and third, fourth and fifth—thoughts as she approached Evan's door Wednesday evening after work. She'd spent a little too much time getting ready that morning, finally settling on a cherry-red sweater and dark pants that were both professional and flattering. She carried a roomy leather tote bag that held a folder full of materials about establishing scholarships, just in case Evan and Tate were interested in what she'd learned through her research.

After much deliberation, she had decided not to tell Lucy what she was doing this evening. This was the only day of the week when it would be possible to get away with the omission. The eye clinic was open until six on Wednesdays, an hour later than usual. Lucy picked up Leslie and Daniel from school, fed them an early dinner, then took them to church where she had Bible study and choir practice, and the twins attended kids' Bible classes and children's choir. They were never home until almost eight, so Renae took that evening as Mom's night out, shopping or getting a manicure, sometimes meeting friends for dinner or a movie, other times just going home to read in rare, uninterrupted peace.

She wondered now if she should have gone home to read tonight.

She had announced her arrival downstairs and Evan had buzzed her in, so it was too late to cancel, though at least half a dozen times in the past few days she had reached for her phone to do just that. She had resisted the impulses only by refusing to allow herself to think about Evan and the past. She'd stayed busy with the life she'd made for herself, preparing for this appointment as she would any business meeting, and the days had flown past. Now she found herself standing in the hallway outside his apartment, not at all sure she was ready to see Evan again.

At least Tate would be there to defuse the tension, she reminded herself firmly. While Tate had also been a friend of Jason's, he and Renae had no personal baggage between them. If he was still as chatty and jovial as he'd been back then, there should be few uncomfortable silences. She would keep the conversation focused on the scholarship and then they would go their own ways again.

Evan opened the door before she could even knock. "Renae. Hi, come in."

He smiled at her as he invited her inside, and her pulse rate fluttered crazily in response.

So much for keeping her unwanted reactions to sexy Evan Daugherty firmly under control.

Chapter Two

Holding her head high and keeping her smile as relaxed as possible considering the chaos inside her, Renae stepped past Evan, looking around his home as she entered. The furnishings were tasteful—minimal, but nicely accented with plants. No surprise there, since that was Evan's career specialty.

"Very nice," she said, moving to admire the panorama of the north bank of the Arkansas River and the Little Rock skyline on the other side. The swirling river water reflected the deepening blue sky and mirrored the trees splashed with fall color. The scenery brightened up the beige-on-beige decor inside Evan's apartment.

"I have to admit that view is why I chose this place."

She realized Evan had stepped next to her to admire the panorama, standing so close that an unguarded movement would cause their arms to touch. While she did not suspect he meant anything by the proximity other than affable view-sharing, she still moved away. "Something smells good."

He remained where he was, keeping a respectable distance between them. "I picked up dinner on the way here. I hope you still like pizza."

"Doesn't everyone?" Ignoring his implication that he remembered her fondness for pizza, she glanced toward the other end of the room. Three flat boxes sat on a dining table on the other side of a low serving bar, next to plates, napkins, flatware and a stack of papers she assumed to be scholarship materials. "Three pizzas? Just how many people are on this committee?"

"Three," he admitted rather sheepishly. "I wasn't sure what toppings you like, so I got an assortment. I'll dine on the leftovers for a few days."

"When it comes to pizza, I'm not picky."

"Can I get you something to drink while we wait for Tate? Or we could dig in and let him catch up when he gets here. I know your time is limited."

His cell phone buzzed before she could answer. "That's Tate," he said with a glance at the screen. "There are drinks in the fridge, glasses set out on the counter. Help yourself while I find out what's keeping him."

She had just poured diet cola over ice when Evan joined her in the kitchen. She could tell by his expression what he was going to say even before he spoke.

"I'm sorry, but something has come up and Tate can't make it. Looks like it's just you and me."

Renae swallowed hard and set the soda can down with a thump.

It flashed through her mind that Lucy would surely accuse Evan of arranging this so he would have Renae alone. Renae rejected that possibility as soon as it occurred to her. Judging by Evan's expression, he was just as dismayed as she was that they wouldn't have Tate as a buffer.

He must have seen the reservations in her eyes. "If you'd rather reschedule when Tate can join us…"

She shook her head, telling herself she was being foolish. Keeping her expression schooled and her voice brisk, she picked up her glass and moved toward the table. "Since I'm here, let's take a look at what you have. I brought some information about other private scholarship programs, if you'd be interested in seeing it."

He nodded cordially, matching her impersonal tone. "Yes, of course. Have a seat and help yourself to pizza, and we'll go through the notes Tate and I have compiled so far."

She sank into one of the four chairs at the slate-topped, bar-height table, hoping he would sit across from her, well out of accidental touching distance. Instead, he chose the place to her right, pulling a pizza box and a stack of papers toward them.

All too aware of how close he sat, of his elbow almost brushing hers when he moved, of the way he looked at her every time she glanced his way, she reached quickly for a file folder.

As he had warned her, the progress thus far was somewhat haphazard. At this point, the award was only a thousand dollars, but that helped with books and supplies. Evan and Tate had paid the scholarship out of their own pockets for the one check they had awarded thus far, but they'd started an account for future donations. They'd had several modest contributions from friends and associates. Financially, the program seemed to be off to a fair start, though Evan admitted they'd had little time to initiate fundraising efforts. He'd thought about sending out a letter to their old friends from high school and college, but he wasn't very good at composing those things, he admitted.

"I can draft the letter," Renae offered, making a note on the pad she'd opened beside her. She seemed to have stepped in as secretary of this informal committee, but that was fine with her. It played to her particular strengths and made her feel that she made a valuable contribution to the cause—and most of her input could be through email, she couldn't help thinking.

Keeping her gaze on the paperwork, she listened to Evan's explanation of the direction he and Tate had in mind for the scholarship and offered a few suggestions of her own. He was very receptive to her ideas, making annotations of his own to share with Tate later, and she was gratified by how open he was to her input.

The first recipient of the Jason Sanchez Memorial Scholarship had been nineteen-year-old Stuart O'Hara, who had since become newlywed Tate's brother-in-law. There had been no formal application—Tate had offered Stuart the scholarship on an impulse when the young man had announced that he would not be attending college because of finances and other family issues. Evan had gone along because he and Tate had been discussing the establishment of a scholarship anyway, and he figured it was time to get started.

When Renae saw how seriously the young man was taking the honor, she felt a bit more comfortable with the nepotism of that first award. Evan had printed out three emails Stuart had sent about his academic progress that semester, each ending with a repetition of his gratitude for their assistance.

"He has an academic scholarship paying for his tuition and a student loan to cover living expenses, but this thousand-dollar award for books and supplies seems to mean a lot to him," Evan explained. "I think it's because he was on the verge of not attending college at all when Tate offered him our scholarship as a sign of faith in him. He was at a point in his life when he needed to hear that, I guess. Apparently, there were some family issues holding him back. But he seems to have committed himself completely to making a success of college. That's why he keeps emailing us about his grades, even though he's only been in school a couple of months. Tate's actually had to remind him to make a little time for fun."

"Stuart sounds like a good kid," Renae said, glancing again at the grateful notes.

Evan nodded. "I haven't actually met him, but from what Tate has told me, he is."

She should have known better than to meet his eyes. Their gazes held, and she felt a shiver of awareness course through her. It had been too long since she'd been near an attractive man, too long since she had felt physical awareness warm her blood.

She forced her attention back to her notes. Was she really so starved for a man's attention? How foolish.

Sure, she was young and there were times when she longed for a man's touch. She'd told herself she would date again, once the twins were a little older and her schedule a bit less hectic. In the meantime, her life was almost perfect just as it was, she reminded herself firmly. She had no intention of doing anything to change that. Most especially with Evan Daugherty, who had already caused her more than enough heartache and confusion.

To distract herself, she stayed focused on the conversation. "Okay, so I'll start putting together an application form to send to local schools and to make available on the website you and Tate are working on. We still need to draft a more formal statement of the qualifications we're looking for in our applicants."

Though Stuart attended a small, private college in Missouri, Evan and Tate had decided it would be easier to limit future awards to students in Arkansas, and Renae agreed. They would choose two recipients for next year, in addition to renewing Stuart's award, but eventually they hoped to spread the assistance to even more young scholars. Maybe even increase the award amount to cover more than books and supplies, if they were successful with their fundraising efforts.

"We can draft the statement and make some more decisions at our next meeting. Since all the materials are here, we might as well just keep my apartment as our meeting place. Would there be any time you could meet next week?"

"Next week?" she asked with a little frown.

He nodded, studying her face. "Tate should be able to join us then. He wanted to be here today, but his wife's car wouldn't start and she was stranded at work. Tate had to pick up their daughter at day care, then arrange to have the battery in her car replaced."

"They have a daughter?" Though she knew Tate was a newlywed, this was the first she had heard about a child.

"Her name is Daryn. She's about a year old. Tate

married a single mom. He met Kim when the baby was only a couple months old, right after she went back to work after her maternity leave. They had sort of a whirlwind romance and surprised everyone with a sudden marriage. It's pretty amusing how they got together, actually. Maybe he'll tell you about it next week."

Again, Evan was making the supposition that she would meet with him again next week.

He must have read the hesitation in her expression because he added, "Is next week too soon? I understand if you can't arrange a sitter for the kids again so quickly. Maybe you would rather Tate and I handle this from now on and email you?"

That was exactly what she should do. But she really didn't want to be left out of this project now that she'd become so emotionally invested in seeing it succeed.

She shook her head. "No, if we're going to get everything in place to start accepting applications for next fall, we should probably meet again soon. Next Wednesday will work for me."

She assumed each meeting with Evan would get easier, especially since he had cooperated with her in keeping the tone between them strictly business. And in the meantime, she would decide whether it was time to let Lucy know about these meetings. She couldn't say she was looking forward to that, but she was reluctant to deceive her mother-in-law, even through omission.

Evan insisted that she leave the dinner cleanup to him. She gathered her notes and stuffed them into her bag in preparation to leave.

He glanced at his watch as he walked with her into the living room. "I'm sure you're eager to get home to the kids. Do you have a regular sitter for them?"

"Lucy takes care of them when I'm not home. They always have activities at church on Wednesday evenings, which gives me one free night a week on my own. That's why I'm available to meet with you and Tate next Wednesday."

"Lucy." Evan cleared his throat uncomfortably after repeating the name. "You mean Lucy Sanchez?"

She nodded, understanding why his tone had suddenly changed. It hadn't occurred to her until just then that Evan probably wasn't aware of her living arrangements. "Jason's mother."

"She still lives close by, I take it."

"Actually, she lives with us. After Jason died, she took early retirement from her job with the Revenue Department and moved in with me during the last couple months of my pregnancy. She stayed to help with the twins when we brought them home from the hospital. When we saw how well it was working out, she sold her little house and we've shared a home since. It's been an almost-ideal arrangement for all of us."

She could tell he was startled to hear that she and Lucy shared a home. He wouldn't be the first person to find it odd that a thirty-year-old widow chose to live with her mother-in-law for seven years after her husband's death, with no plans to change the situation. Renae rarely bothered to explain and never made excuses. It was a choice that suited her family, and she had no qualms about saying so.

Evan pushed his hands into his pockets, his expression shuttered, his brown eyes darker than usual. "Does she still spit on the ground every time she hears my name?"

She didn't really know how to answer that only partially facetious question. She settled for, "Not quite that bad."

A muscle flickered in his set jaw. "Okay, but does she still blame me for Jason's death?"

Renae sighed wearily and pushed a strand of blond hair behind her ear. "She still grieves for her son. She gets caught up in 'if only.' If only he hadn't gone riding that day, if only he hadn't bought a bike in the first place...that sort of thing."

"All of which lead back to blaming me."

She was unable to argue. It seemed best to take her leave then, instead. "Thank you for the pizza, and for letting me be a part of establishing the scholarship."

He nodded and walked her to the door. They reached for the knob at the same time, his hand landing on top of hers. Rather than moving it immediately, he went still, his fingers warm around hers. His face was somber when he looked down at her. "Renae?"

Her heart was racing much faster than it should have been, especially considering they were barely making contact. Yet that touch of skin on skin, the warmth that radiated from him, the nearness and strength of him— all sent her thoughts winging back to a stolen kiss on a dark, summer night. A kiss that had left her bewildered, conflicted and crying into her pillow for several nights afterward. A kiss that still brought up feelings of guilt and confusion on the very rare occasion when she allowed herself to remember it.

"What?" she whispered, unable to pull away just yet.

"Do *you* still blame me?"

She didn't know if he referred to the kiss or to Jason's accident, but her reply applied to both. "I try not to let myself dwell on the past."

That muscle twitched again in his jaw. "That's not really an answer."

She drew her hand from under his, moving away so that no contact remained between them. "Jason made his own decisions."

Just as she had made hers.

She shifted restlessly toward the door, making it clear she wanted Evan to open it. Without further delay, he did so. "I'll see you next week," he said as she walked out.

She merely nodded and kept walking. Perhaps she should find an excuse to handle the rest of their scholarship business through the safely impersonal distance of email after all.

"You're quieter than usual today, Evan. Is something wrong?"

Resting his chopsticks against his plate, Evan shook his head and reached for his teacup.

"Just hungry," he explained in response to Lynette Price's concerned question from across the restaurant table. "I overslept this morning, so I had to gulp down an apple for breakfast on the way to a client meeting."

Lynette nodded as if that fully explained his introspection. "I hate when that happens. I forgot to set my alarm last Friday and I was fifteen minutes late to work. Threw me off schedule for the rest of the day."

A week after Evan's meeting with Renae, he and four friends had gathered for their every-Wednesday lunch at a Little Rock restaurant. His business partner, Tate Price, sat on the opposite side of the table flanked by his bride, Kim Banks Price, and Tate's sister, Lynette

Price. To Evan's right sat Emma Grainger, who worked with Kim and Lynette.

Lynette, a physical therapist, and her coworker friends had started the Wednesday lunch outings almost a year ago. Lynette had invited her brother and Evan to join them a few weeks later. That was when Tate had met Kim. Now Tate and Kim were newly married.

Though Tate and Kim's wedding had been a spur-of-the-moment event, none of the others had been particularly surprised when they paired off. Sparks had flown between them from the start, though it seemed that the couple had been the last to acknowledge the attraction between them.

"I'm sorry I caused Tate to miss your scholarship meeting last week," Kim said to Evan.

"It wasn't your fault your car wouldn't start," he assured her.

Evan remembered how hesitant he'd been to tell Renae that Tate had to cancel. He had sensed that she had been more comfortable at the thought of meeting with both of them rather than with Evan alone. He'd done his best to set her at ease, and he thought he'd succeeded for the most part—with the exception of their rather emotional parting.

He still didn't know for certain if Renae held resentment toward him for Jason's death. After all, it had taken several years for him to stop blaming himself. Being outright accused at the funeral by Jason's grieving mother had certainly not helped him with that slow healing.

"How was your meeting with Mrs. Sanchez?" Emma asked curiously. Like the others, she'd heard about the scholarship launch, and had been told that the widow of the man in whose honor it was established wanted to be involved.

It still rather startled Evan to think of Renae as Mrs. Sanchez, a name he associated with Jason's mother. Renae had been so young when she and Jason married, and not much older when she'd been widowed. She was still young, for that matter, and yet she lived quietly with her children and her mother-in-law. Was she still in mourning for Jason?

"It went well," he said, keeping his thoughts to himself. "We made some decisions, outlined some of the things we need to do next."

"Is there anything I can do to help?" Kim offered. "I'm still so grateful to you both for making my brother your first recipient."

"He wouldn't have gotten it if he hadn't been deserving," Evan reminded her, not for the first time. "I'll let you know if there's anything you can do."

"I'd like to help, too," Lynette offered. "Maybe we can come up with an idea for a fundraiser."

Evan nodded. "That would be good."

"We'll all help," Emma said. "It's definitely a worthy cause. But I'd like to hear more about Jason Sanchez. You guys haven't told us much about him, other than that he was a high school teacher who died in a motorcycle accident. What was he like?"

Evan and Tate exchanged glances, and Evan was sure memories were flashing through Tate's mind, just as they were his own.

"Jason was great," Evan said finally. "Smart, funny, outgoing. Every kid's favorite teacher in school, you know? He made a real effort to keep his classes interesting, to bring history to life for his students. He'd only been teaching a couple years when he died, so I guess you could say he hadn't had time to burn out yet."

"He wanted to teach college history," Tate contributed. "He liked academia, enjoyed the challenges and even the politics of it all."

Evan nodded. A good-looking guy, Jason had savored being the center of attention, knew he was admired by his female students, fancied himself in the role of popular professor. His dad had died when Jason was a young teen, leaving him an only child to be pampered and indulged by his adoring mother.

Several years his junior, a lonely young woman with a deep-seated longing for family and stability, Renae Ingle had fallen under Jason's spell while she was an occupational therapy student and Jason was studying for his master's degree. Evan had been doing an internship in urban gardening in Chicago that year. By the time he returned home, Renae and Jason were a couple.

Which made it all the more wrong when Evan had fallen for Renae himself.

"You knew him from childhood?" Emma persisted.

"I did," Evan confirmed with a nod. "Jason and I became friends in junior high and remained close after that. I met Tate in college, where we were both studying landscape design. I introduced him to Jason and the three of us spent a lot of time together after that."

"Jason was a good friend," Tate agreed. "We had some fun times, didn't we, Ev?"

Evan nodded.

"I saw Jason a couple of times when he stopped by the house on his motorcycle to meet up with Tate and Evan," Lynette volunteered. "He was really good-looking, had a smile that made my teen knees melt. I had such a crush on him, and I think he knew it."

"Did you ever meet his wife?" Emma asked.

Lynette shook her head. "No. The guys weren't hanging out as much when Jason started dating her."

Tate shrugged. "We got busy. I was working for a landscape design company in Dallas, Evan was away doing an internship, Jason was getting his master's degree. Then Evan went into the army, Jason and Renae got married, and Jason started teaching and studying for his doctorate. After that, we were lucky to all be in the same town for an afternoon to shoot some hoops or ride our…"

Tate's words faded. Obviously he had suddenly remembered that final motorcycle ride Jason and Evan had taken. "Anyway," he continued quickly, "Evan spent more time with Jason and Renae when they were dating, before he went off to the army, so he knows her better than I do."

Evan still clearly remembered Jason introducing him to Renae. Shaking his hand, she had gazed up at him with a smile in those vivid blue eyes and Evan had felt his heart take a hard flop in his chest. Clichéd, maybe, but true. During the next few months, he'd spent some time with Jason and Renae, even double-dating on a few occasions, though his own dates hadn't led anywhere. Maybe because he'd had a hard time taking his attention from Renae whenever she was in the vicinity though he'd done his best to ignore his attraction to her.

There had been times when he thought he'd sensed an answering awareness in her when their eyes had met, but he'd tried to convince himself he was only projecting. It had been easier for his peace of mind to believe he had no chance with his buddy's girlfriend, and he thought Renae had made an equally determined effort to ignore the sparks between them. Until the night they had found themselves alone in a pretty little garden at a friend's house, standing beside a moonlit fountain.

"Jason has asked me to marry him," barely twenty-one-year-old Renae had confided tentatively, her face young and vulnerable in the pale light as she had gazed up at Evan.

He'd felt his stomach twist, even as his fingers tightened around the beer can in his hand. He'd downed a few too many at that gathering to celebrate Jason's master's degree in education. Yet he found Renae's eyes more intoxicating than the beverage as he asked in a gravelly voice, "What did you tell him?"

Glancing downward, she had hesitated, moistening her lips and nervously tucking a strand of long, bleached hair behind her ear. "I told him I'd think about it."

Evan used his free hand to lift her chin so that he could look hard at her expression, as if he could read her thoughts in her glittering eyes. "Do you want to marry Jason?"

"I've been alone a long time," she had whispered. "Jason and Lucy love me and want me to be a part of their family."

Lucy had been all in favor of Jason marrying Renae. There had been times when Evan had wondered even back then if Lucy had pushed the match even harder than Jason had. Though Jason had seemed oblivious, maybe Lucy had sensed Evan's attraction to Renae. Maybe that was part of the reason Lucy had been so cool toward him before Jason's death, and downright hostile afterward.

"That's not what I asked you," he had growled. He'd told himself he was asking for Jason's sake, not his own. "Do you want to marry him?"

"I—" She had paused with a hard swallow before saying, "I think I do."

Evan had felt his heart drop. His first reaction had been pain—his second, an illogical anger.

"Well, let me be the first to kiss the bride," he'd said on a beer-fueled impulse. And he had pressed his lips to Renae's, intending nothing more than a brief, forbidden, curiosity-satisfying kiss.

It had instantly flared into so much more.

"I'm sure Mrs. Sanchez is pleased that you guys want to memorialize her husband with this scholarship."

Emma's comment brought Evan abruptly back to the present. Realizing he had been staring at the noodles on his plate for several frozen moments, he stabbed his chopsticks into the pile, avoiding Emma's entirely too-perceptive dark eyes. "Yes, she seems to be. Tate and I will tell her this evening that the three of you want to be involved with fundraising. I'm sure she'll be touched."

To his relief, Tate changed the subject then with a funny story about something little Daryn had done the night before. Though Evan participated in the conversation, he still found himself drifting back to that night so long ago, to a kiss that had flared into a hungry, passionate embrace that had almost burned out of control before Renae had broken it off with a shocked gasp.

Staring up at him with tear-filled eyes, she had asked in a choked voice, "What was that?"

"Something I've been wanting to do for weeks," he had admitted grimly. "But if you're going to marry Jason, it will never happen again."

"He loves me," she had whispered, wringing her hands and looking at Evan with raw vulnerability. "Can you give me any reason I shouldn't marry him?"

Evan had felt the words trembling on his lips. But then he'd stared down at the crushed aluminum can in his hand and asked himself what in the hell he was doing. Jason was his friend. And Evan had plans that did not yet include marriage or children.

Renae was young, confused, maybe suffering cold feet at the thought of major commitment, but he knew she cared deeply for Jason. He would do nothing more to come between them.

"I'm sure you'll both be very happy," he had said as he'd turned to walk away without looking back. A month later, he'd been in boot camp, and Renae had been wearing a diamond on her left hand.

For a long time afterward, he had wondered what Renae would have said if he'd told her that Jason wasn't the only one who loved her.

That was something he would never know, he reminded himself as he finished his lunch with his friends. Too much had happened since, too many reasons for him to keep his distance—not the least of which included her mother-in-law who blamed him still for Jason's death.

Chapter Three

"Renae." Holding her right hand in his, Tate greeted her with a warm smile Wednesday evening. "It's so good to see you. You look great."

She returned the smile, noting that time had made few changes in him. Though his cheerful, guy-next-door good looks had never affected her in quite the same way as Evan's darker, more solemn appeal, she had always liked Tate. "It's nice to see you again, too, Tate. Congratulations on your new marriage."

He grinned. "Thanks. I got lucky. I have a beautiful wife and an adorable little girl who's almost a year old. Want to see a picture?"

Standing nearby, Evan shook his head. "You're in for it now, Renae. Tate whips out those photos every chance he gets."

Rather charmed by Tate's enthusiasm for his family, Renae assured him that she would love to see the photo. She smiled when he handed her his phone, on which was displayed a sweet snapshot of an attractive, honey-haired woman and a laughing baby.

"This must be your wife."

"Yes. Kim. And the baby is Daryn. The next picture is a close-up of Daryn."

Renae dutifully admired several more shots, then returned the phone to Tate. "You have a lovely family."

"Thanks. They're hanging out with Lynette this evening, watching a chick flick on TV—though I imagine Daryn will expect them to pay more attention to her than the movie. What about you? Do you have photos of the twins on you?"

After only a split-second hesitation, Renae handed her phone to Tate. Evan moved closer to look over Tate's shoulder at the duo displayed on the little screen.

"Wow." After studying the photo, Tate lifted his eyes to Renae. "Your son is a carbon copy of Jason."

She nodded. "Yes. If you set their first-grade photos side by side, you can hardly tell them apart."

"Leslie looks very much like him, too," Evan observed quietly. "Definitely has his eyes."

"They both do," she agreed.

She slipped her phone back into the pocket of the black slacks she wore with a gray-and-black-striped sweater. Though she'd been told the twins shared many of her mannerisms, and that both had her smile, she knew there was little physical resemblance between them. They had inherited Jason's near-black hair and eyes rather than her blond, blue-eyed looks. She saw him so often in them, as she knew Lucy did, and the resemblance comforted them both, letting them feel that Jason lived on in the children he'd never had the chance to meet.

Just as his memory would live on in this scholarship in his name, she thought, reminding herself firmly of the reason they were all here now.

"I brought the donation request letter for the two of you to look over," she said, digging into her bag. "If you have any recommendations, feel free to let me know."

Seeming to understand that she needed to bring the topic back to the present, Evan moved toward the table. "Let's get comfortable. We've got deli sandwiches this time. Turkey or veggie on whole wheat with fruit cups and chocolate chip cookies for dessert. Help yourself. I'll get drinks. Iced tea, soda or bottled water?"

"You don't have to keep supplying food, Evan," Renae said even as she took a seat and reached for a plate and a sandwich.

He shrugged as he set a glass in front of her. "I'm always hungry after work and I figured you might be, too. Let's see that letter."

As Renae had expected, it was a little easier having Tate to defuse some of the tension between her and Evan. The undertones were still there, though she hoped Tate was unaware of them. Maybe they were all in her own mind, but still she was grateful to Tate for his easy chatter and ready laughs while they made several big decisions about the scholarship fund.

Only forty-five minutes after they'd gathered, Tate glanced at his watch and pushed away from the table. "Sorry to jet, but I've got a late business meeting in Benton in less than an hour. I'd better head out. I'll give you a call later to let you know how it goes, Evan."

"Yeah, thanks."

Renae set down her pen, thinking of the decisions still to be made. "Do you want to meet again next week to talk about the website?"

Standing, Tate reached for his jacket. "I'll be out of town next Wednesday, but I'm fine with whatever arrangements the two of you make. I know we're under pressure to get everything up and running by the beginning of the new semester after Christmas break."

So she and Evan would be alone again next week. Renae cleared her throat and glanced briefly at Evan. "We can wait until the following week when Tate can join us again."

Evan shook his head. "Tate's right. We don't have much longer to get this all ironed out. If you're available, I think we should go ahead and have our meeting."

The scholarship, she reminded herself. That was what was truly important here. "Yes, all right. But I'll bring food next time."

Evan smiled. "If you're sure you have time."

"Later, guys." Tate dashed for the door, snatching a cookie from the table to take with him. Because he had always been casually demonstrative, he brushed a kiss on Renae's cheek on the way past her. It startled her a little, but made her smile nonetheless.

The apartment seemed smaller somehow with Tate gone. More intimate. Definitely quieter.

Renae gathered her notes and stuffed them into her bag. "I guess that's all we can do today. I'll compile that list of state high schools this week so we can start mailing the application forms as soon as we have it printed. We'll start sending the donation requests out at the same time. With the potential donors we've identified, I think we should have a decent response, especially since we're making it clear that no contribution is too small to be appreciated."

Evan seemed to have no issues with her summary of their progress. Once again, she was pleased with how much input he and Tate wanted from her, even though the scholarship had been their idea and was initially being funded by their company.

"We should need only a few more meetings to finalize all the details," he said, "and then we can take a break until we start reading applications in April."

She told herself it would be a good thing when there was no reason to see Evan every week. She found herself thinking of him entirely too often during her days, and rarely solely in connection with scholarship business.

She insisted on helping him clear the table this time, since they'd finished a bit earlier than the week before. She carried glasses into his galley-style kitchen and placed them in the dishwasher, turning just as he entered with the leftover cookies, so that he unintentionally blocked her exit.

"Sorry," he said, setting the cookies on the counter.

She moved to pass him, but he didn't immediately step out of the way, bringing them even closer together.

His gaze held hers when he reached up unexpectedly to brush the ends of her angled bob, his fingertips just brushing her cheek. "Your hair is different," he murmured. "Shorter and darker."

Self-conscious, she shrugged. "I stopped bleaching it. And it's easier to wear it shorter with my busy schedule now."

"It looks good."

Uncertain how to take the compliment, she said merely, "Thank you."

He continued to search her face, as if noting every slight difference. "More than just your hair has changed."

"That's hardly surprising," she answered with forced lightness. "I was just a kid when we met, now I'm a thirty-year-old mother of school-age twins. Of course I've changed."

"You were a pretty girl," he replied. "You're a beautiful woman."

Her eyes closed for just a moment, her cheeks going warm. His simple statement had rocked her to her toes.

"That's one thing that hasn't changed about *you,*" she said, her voice sounding a bit strangled to her own ears. "I still don't know how to respond to some of the things you say."

"It was just an observation," he said, and moved out of her path.

She gathered her things quickly. "I should go. I'll see you next week."

"I'll try not to make you uncomfortable with uninvited accolades."

Though the words could be interpreted as somewhat defensive, he didn't seem to be annoyed. She looked at him from beneath her lashes and saw that his mouth was tilted with a very faint smile. Which made her feel a little foolish for overreacting to what he had apparently considered a simple compliment.

What was it about Evan that made her so often feel like such a fool around him?

She moved toward the door. "Next week," she repeated, vowing she would have herself firmly under control by then.

"Renae?" His voice stopped her just as she reached for the doorknob.

"Yes?" she asked without turning around.

"I miss him, too."

Once again, he had floored her with a few simple words. Unable to respond, she merely nodded and opened the door, stepping through it and closing it quickly behind her.

Sitting in her car a few minutes later, she gripped the top of the steering wheel and rested her forehead against her hands, remembering Evan's words. His tone had been sincere, and his voice had held an old pain she believed was genuine. Whatever still simmered between her and Evan, Evan did miss his friend.

She reminded herself that their one impetuous kiss hadn't exactly been a betrayal of Jason, especially since they'd walked away quickly and had never allowed themselves to be alone together again after that. It hadn't been long afterward, in fact, that Evan had joined the army, saying he wanted to make a contribution to the war against terrorism that had been raging so furiously then. He'd been home on leave the weekend Jason died.

Even knowing they'd done nothing wrong, she still struggled with old guilt Evan probably couldn't understand. Guilt because she and Jason had parted with an uneasy truce after a quarrel. And guilt because, even though she had been a good wife to Jason and had loved him very much, she'd never been quite sure what she would have done had Evan answered differently when she'd asked him to give her a reason not to marry Jason.

* * *

Thursday evening, Renae sat in an uncomfortable, straight-backed chair in the school auditorium, watching Leslie and Daniel take their bows on stage along with the other first graders who had participated in the program at this month's PTA meeting. Along with the other audience members, Renae clapped heartily, laughing wryly when irrepressible Daniel pumped a fist in satisfaction that the performance was over.

"They did so well," Lucy said, beaming with pride. "I think they were the stars of the show."

Because neither of the twins had been featured singers in the medley of children's tunes the classes had performed, Renae merely smiled.

Janet Caple, a mom who sat at Renae's left, looked her way, still applauding as the players filed noisily off the stage under the direction of the first grade teachers. "They were all great, weren't they? And how cute was it when Mickey Johnson forgot the words to his solo and all the other kids shouted them out for him?"

Renae chuckled. "The twins are looking forward to coming to Jacob's birthday party Saturday, Janet. Thank you for inviting them."

"Jacob wouldn't have it any other way. He loves playing with Daniel and Leslie. I hope you'll plan to stay. I'm providing food for the adults so we can visit while the kids play." Janet angled herself a bit farther forward so she could see Lucy on the other side of Renae. "You're welcome to come, too, Lucy."

"Thank you, Janet, but my Sunday school class is having a luncheon Saturday. Renae will bring the twins to the party."

Janet leaned closer to Renae and lowered her voice

to a conspiratorial murmur. "Mike Bishop is bringing Cooper and Jackson, because it's Mike's weekend to have the kids. He'll probably hang around to chat awhile. He's awfully cute, you know."

Renae felt Lucy shift restlessly in her seat, indicating she'd probably overheard Janet's not-so-subtle attempt at a fix-up. "I've only met him a couple of times, but he seems nice enough."

"His boys are good kids, too. And he and Theresa are long past the divorce, so maybe you should get to know him a little better."

She didn't want to be rude, but she wasn't interested in Janet's matchmaking efforts. Fortunately, Lucy stood then, bringing the conversation to an end. "We'd better get home so the twins can have their baths and get to bed on time, shouldn't we, Renae?"

The school program had been held early in the evening, barely giving Renae time to get home from work before heading out again. Lucy had fed the kids an early dinner, but Renae had opted to wait, so she was a little hungry now.

Tucking her bag beneath her arm, she stood beside her mother-in-law and took her leave of Janet, saying she would see her on Saturday. She hoped her lack of response to Janet's unsubtle hints about Mike Bishop had made her disinterest clear. She would hate for things to get awkward at the birthday party Saturday.

She had enough awkward situations in her life right now.

"I hope you don't let Janet Caple make you uncomfortable at the party Saturday," Lucy said later, as if she'd read the misgivings on Renae's face.

Having just tucked the children into bed, Renae was finally getting a chance to have her dinner, sitting at the table with a freshly warmed bowl of her mother-in-law's delicious beef stew and a wedge of jalapeño corn bread. Lucy's heritage was Argentinean and her late husband had come from Mexico, so peppers were a staple of her cooking. Renae often teased that the twins had developed steel-lined mouths as a result. They loved their food spicy.

"This stew is delicious, as always, Lucy. And I won't be uncomfortable at the party. I always enjoy visiting with the other parents."

"I heard Janet talking to you about that man—that divorced father. I hope she doesn't get too pushy about it."

"I know how to handle matchmakers," Renae answered mildly. "Don't fret about it."

Renae had been on a few dinner dates during the past two years, none of which had been successful enough for follow-up outings. While Lucy was hardly enthusiastic about the idea of Renae dating, she hadn't actively discouraged her, though she'd always seemed relieved when there had been no subsequent contact. Renae didn't believe Lucy had ever dated after losing her own husband, having focused exclusively on her then-teenage son afterward. Since Jason's death, Lucy's world had revolved around Renae and the twins, with her church activities and a couple of close friends her only other interests.

Renae, on the other hand, had her job and a few good friends outside the family with whom she met occasionally for "girls' night out," usually on Wednesday evenings. And yet there were still times when she felt an emptiness in her life outside her family. A longing for something…more. Something those few unsatisfying dinner dates had not provided. She'd often wondered why she couldn't be more like Lucy in being wholly content with all the blessings she had.

Maybe if she were more like Lucy, she wouldn't have been so disconcerted by a simple compliment from a broodingly handsome man yesterday. She wouldn't have lain in her bed afterward reliving the light brush of his fingertips against her cheek, and shivering in response to the memory.

The prospect of spending time with Mike Bishop on Saturday left her completely unmoved. But the thought of next week's scholarship meeting with Evan—well, that made her pulse rate jump measurably.

She didn't even want to consider how Lucy would react to that information.

"That dinner was really good, Renae, though I'm afraid you went to too much trouble. When you said you were providing the food, I assumed you'd get take-out, as I did."

"It was no trouble. I'm glad you enjoyed it," she replied self-consciously to Evan's compliment as she snapped the top back onto the plastic container in which she'd brought a salad made with roasted chicken, Bibb lettuce, cheese cubes, grapes and toasted pecans tossed with a homemade vinaigrette dressing she'd brought in a separate container. She'd provided whole wheat rolls to serve on the side. Though she'd worried that Evan wouldn't find the quick meal hearty enough, he'd appeared to enjoy it, and had eaten two of the small brownies she'd brought for dessert.

She'd made the meal last night. When Lucy had commented about the size of the salad, Renae had merely shrugged and muttered something about "potluck." It hadn't exactly been a lie, she'd assured herself, even though she knew Lucy had assumed the potluck was one of the office luncheons that took place at the clinic.

Evan closed his laptop. "We got a lot done this evening."

"We did. Tate will be proud of us," she replied lightly.

"Yes, he will."

In some ways, these meetings were getting easier, she thought as she stacked her notes and slipped them into her bag. By focusing intently on the scholarship, she and Evan were able to keep their personal issues out of the way. At least outwardly. Inwardly, she still shivered whenever their eyes met, though she hoped she'd done a decent job of hiding that from him.

Evan cleared his throat, seeming to search for an innocuous topic that was not scholarship related. "How are the kids? Looking forward to celebrating Halloween this weekend?"

"Oh, sure. They can't wait to dress up and collect their candy. I'll take them out trick-or-treating while Lucy stays at the house to give out candy."

The mention of Lucy made Evan's smile fade. His eyes were shuttered when he studied her face. "Have you told Lucy you've been meeting with me?"

This time it was she who cleared her throat. She wasn't sure exactly how he'd made that leap, but she wouldn't lie to him. "Um, not exactly. But I will."

It needed to be sooner rather than later. It was going to be hard enough as it was to explain why she had waited so long. Surely Lucy would agree eventually that the scholarship was worth the renewed contact with Evan and Tate.

Evan glanced at the open plastic container on the table. "Tate's going to be sorry he missed this. Best brownies I ever ate."

So he didn't want to talk about Lucy now. Neither did she. Cooperating with the lighter tone, she forced a smile. "I'm glad you like them, but they really are just standard brownies. I made a double batch last night, so there are still plenty at home. I'll leave the rest of these with you. You can share them with Tate or keep them for yourself."

He laughed softly. "Share with Tate? No way. He missed out today. These are mine."

Her stomach did a somersault in response to his laugh. She was entranced by the deep, warm sound of it, and the way it lightened his brown eyes and softened his firm mouth. It had been a very long time since she'd heard Evan laugh. She'd almost forgotten the effect it had always had on her.

She stood. "I hope you'll enjoy them."

"I know I will," he said, rising with her.

He walked her to the door, where he smiled down at her. "Have fun with the kids this weekend. Maybe you can show me pictures of their costumes next week."

"I'd be happy to."

"Thanks again for the brownies. And I didn't even have to say 'trick or treat.'"

She chuckled, smiling up at him. "Happy Halloween, Evan." He focused on her mouth. She wondered if this was the first time she'd truly smiled at him since he'd shown up in her life again. Probably.

She thought maybe he intended to simply brush his

lips across her cheek. A casually friendly parting, similar to the way Tate had left her last week. But the undercurrents between Evan and her had never been casual. His mouth touched her cheek, lingered, slid closer to her lips. Holding her breath, she froze, closed her eyes... then turned her head just that fraction of an inch so that their lips met.

It had been so long since she'd savored the slight roughness of a man's face against her skin. Since she had felt warmth radiating from a hard body next to hers, or caught just the faintest whiff of masculine soap and aftershave. Since she had allowed herself to sink into a kiss and turn off everything except the sensations ricocheting inside her. And yet, as much as she had missed those things, she hadn't been truly tempted to throw all caution to the wind and give in to those urges for a long time.

Not until Evan Daugherty had sauntered back into her life.

The kiss didn't last long. Nor did it flare out of control, though Renae was aware, as she was sure Evan was, how easily it could have done so. He didn't try to hold her when she drew away, but kept his arms at his sides, his gaze locked on her face. He could probably see the pulse hammering in her throat and the flush on her cheeks, but she wasn't sure what he saw in her eyes.

"I'll see you next week," he said. Was there just a hint of question in his statement?

She moistened her lips, fancying she could still taste him. Because she couldn't make any promises just then about next week—not until she could think clearly again—she merely nodded shortly and turned to let herself out.

She would be back, she thought in resignation as she made the short drive home. The question that nagged at her now was whether the scholarship was still her only reason for spending time with Evan.

She was playing with fire. And terrified that she would be burned again, no matter how hard she tried to protect herself.

The temperature Saturday evening was cool, but not so cold that the children had to wear coats over the Halloween costumes they'd chosen so carefully. They had both decided to be superheroes this year, so capes and masks and tights had been donned—Daniel in black and electric-blue, Leslie in red and navy. They bounced impatiently while Renae took pictures, then dashed out the door with their plastic, pumpkin-shaped candy pails as soon as Renae gave them permission.

She followed closely behind them as they dashed down the street from door to door. Their little house was on a cul-de-sac in a safe neighborhood, with most of the other houses occupied by young families with children, so almost all the porch lights were on, signaling that trick-or-treaters were welcome. Hanging back, Renae chatted with other parents she knew through their kids. Some of the other parents had dressed in costume, but she had settled for jeans and a black sweatshirt with a Halloween scene on the front.

Daniel soon found his friends, brothers Cooper and Jackson Bishop, who were dressed as police officers. Their dad, Mike, followed behind his sons dressed as a convict in black-and-white stripes and dragging a plastic ball and chain.

Renae smiled at Mike while the kids greeted each

other and showed off their costumes. "Looks like you've been caught."

Lightly kicking the plastic ball, Mike laughed. "Yeah. The boys chose our costumes, needless to say. They thought this was real funny."

"You do look funny, Mr. Bishop," Leslie said, looking up at him with a giggle.

He scowled ferociously. "I'm supposed to look like a scary convict."

She giggled again. "You don't look scary."

"Come on, Leslie, let's go," Daniel ordered impatiently. At a nod from their parents, the twins and the Bishop boys dashed toward the door of a yellow-sided house decorated with white garbage-bag ghosts hanging from the porch.

Mike nodded indulgently after them. "They're having a great time, aren't they? Remember how magical Halloween seemed to be when we were kids? Costumes and make-believe and bags full of candy?"

She had a few fond memories of Halloweens with her cousins. And Jason had loved Halloween, throwing big costume parties every year. He would have so enjoyed taking the twins out trick-or-treating, she thought wistfully. She wanted very much to believe that, despite his mounting reservations in the months before he'd died, he'd have adapted to the demands of fatherhood and what he'd begun to see as the constraints of marriage. He would have fallen in love with the twins, just as she had, and would surely have agreed that no sacrifice was too great for them.

Jason was not like her father, she told herself as she had so many times before when doubts had crept into the back of her mind. He would never have left his children to be raised by others while he was off pursuing his own interests.

"Renae? Did I say something wrong?"

She forced a bright smile for Mike's benefit. "Of course not. I'm just enjoying watching the kids."

"Mom, look what we got!" Daniel held up his pumpkin bucket to display his latest candies. "That lady gave us each a whole handful."

"That was very generous of her," Renae said gravely.

"C'mon, Daniel, the next house is giving out candy bars!"

Turning in response to Cooper's urging, Daniel dashed after the other children to the next house.

Renae glanced up at Mike with a wry smile. "We spend most of their lives trying to limit their sweets and teach them healthy eating habits, then one night a year we let them gather as much candy as they can carry."

Mike laughed. "Theresa and I agreed that the boys get two pieces of candy a day until it's gone. I keep part of it at my place and they take the rest to hers. They eat all their favorite stuff first and forget about the rest, which we finally throw out."

Renae admired the way Mike and his ex maintained cordial relations for the sake of their sons. He really was a nice man. And he'd been flirting with her since the party at Janet's house. She had no doubt that she had only to give him a subtle hint and he would ask her out. But nice as he was, she had no interest at all in giving that sign.

She really was an idiot.

They walked together during the remainder of the leisurely outing, Renae following a few steps behind when Mike teased and carried on with the kids. Daniel obviously loved the attention from his friends' dad. Daniel was at the age when he needed interaction with men, something Renae tried her best to provide through Tae Kwon Do lessons and playdates with friends whose fathers made time to play with them.

The final stop was the house next door to Renae's. Widowed sisters Daisy Sinclair and Maxine Whelan, both in their early seventies, had moved in there a couple years earlier and had become fast friends with Lucy, though the sisters were several years older than her. The three women played dominoes every Thursday evening, which was Lucy's equivalent of Renae's "mom's evening out."

Daisy had a forty-something son serving overseas in a diplomatic post; Maxine had no children. Having no grandchildren of their own, both of them loved the twins and spoiled them shamelessly.

"This is where we say good-night," Renae informed Mike. "We're going to stop in here for a short visit with our neighbors before we go home. It was nice seeing you tonight, Mike."

"Yeah, you, too, Renae. Maybe we'll see each other again soon?"

It was as broad a hint as he'd given her yet. She kept her smile friendly without being particularly encouraging. "I'm sure we'll run into each other at the school. Good night, Mike."

He nodded in resignation. "See you later, Daniel and Leslie. Enjoy the rest of your Halloween."

"Thanks, Mr. Bishop," Daniel said.

As had been arranged previously, Daisy and Maxine invited Renae and the twins in for hot chocolate and homemade cookies to finish off their outing. Waving goodbye to Cooper and Jackson, they entered happily. Having just given out the last of their candy, Lucy walked over to join them for this end-of-Halloween-evening celebration.

Chattering excitedly, the twins showed their grandmother the candy they'd collected, telling her stories about all the friends they'd seen and what everyone had worn and how funny Mike had been as he'd accompanied them. Daisy and Maxine sat them at the little round kitchen table with marshmallow-topped mugs of cocoa and a plate of oversize sugar cookies decorated with brightly colored frosting to resemble smiling jack-o'-lanterns. Renae insisted the twins have no more than one each.

"They're big cookies," she said when they frowned. "One cookie and the hot chocolate is plenty of dessert for tonight."

She knew the sisters would send cookies home with them. Between that and the haul of candy, she would be portioning out sweets for the next month—and would then have to start all over for the next round of holidays.

Maxine picked up a tray holding steaming, fragrant mugs of chamomile tea and four cookies. "We older ladies will have ours in the living room," she told the kids. "Call out if you need anything."

Renae blinked rapidly.

Daisy chuckled in response to what she must have seen on Renae's face. "She didn't mean you, of course, dear. She was talking about the rest of us older ladies."

Renae managed a strained smile and followed them into the living room. Accepting her tea and cookie, she took a seat by the large-screen television on which the sisters watched their many favorite programs. Because it was currently turned off, the screen was dark, and she could see her own reflection there.

She had to drag her eyes away.

Despite being the mother of first graders and a widow for almost seven years, she was only thirty years old. That was still young, she reminded herself fiercely, especially in comparison to the other women in the room. Was she really ready to live the same way they did—content with work and family and household chores and television? Shouldn't there be more? Fun? Excitement?

Passion?

Was it wrong of her to feel this way when she had so many wonderful things in her life? Was she tempting fate to take something away when she still wished for more?

She closed her eyes for a moment, and she could almost feel Evan's mouth against hers again. Could feel her heart racing in her chest, a flush of arousal on her cheeks, a shiver of awareness deep inside her belly. The memory made her feel young again. Desirable. Hungry for something more than a Halloween cookie.

Mike Bishop's flirting hadn't made her feel anything like that.

From the kitchen came a spate of sugar-fueled chatter. At the same time, she heard Lucy laugh musically at something one of the other women had said. Her eyes opened and she frowned hard at that hazy reflection on the television.

She had so very much to lose, if she wasn't very careful.

Standing outside Evan's door on the Wednesday after Halloween, Renae drew a deep breath and smoothed her hands down the sides of the long-sleeved, snugly fitted, brown-and-rust knit dress she had worn to work that day. Though she usually wore pants, she did occasionally wear dresses, so her coworkers hadn't expressed surprise.

Now she wondered if she should have just donned her usual sweater and pants that morning, rather than this admittedly flattering dress. She adjusted the deep cowl neckline, smoothed her hair—then dropped her hand, chiding herself for her primping.

So she'd wanted to look good today for Evan and Tate, she told herself impatiently. She was honest enough with herself to admit that it was probably because her ego was still stinging from Maxine's innocent faux pas. There was no need to stand here second-guessing her choice of clothing when the guys were waiting for her to get the meeting started.

Evan opened the door to her. His gaze swept her and she knew he hadn't missed a detail of her appearance. The appreciation in his expression when he met her eyes again made her feel that the extra few minutes she'd taken that morning had been worth the effort, even as a ripple of nerves and awareness coursed through her.

"You look very nice," Evan said, his voice sounding a bit deeper than usual.

"Thank you."

He, of course, looked as appealing as always, though he was dressed very much as usual in a blue shirt and dark slacks. She stepped past him in the apartment, glancing around the living room. "Tate's not here yet?"

"Tate's not coming."

She turned to Evan in question, trying to read his expression. "Why not?"

He pushed his hands into his pockets. "I told him there was no need, that you and I could handle everything for now."

Renae swallowed hard. Had Evan simply been giving Tate a chance to concentrate on other business—or had he wanted to be alone with her again today?

"I picked up a bucket of chicken on the way home. I hope that's okay with you."

She wasn't in the least bit hungry. "Of course."

He didn't turn directly toward the table. Instead, he simply stood there. Looking at her.

She wasn't sure which of them moved first. Who leaned forward, who reached out. One minute they were on separate sides of the room, the next they were wrapped around each other, their mouths fused in a kiss that melted her spine.

Chapter Four

Renae felt the outline of firm abs beneath Evan's shirt, the breadth of the masculine chest against which her breasts pressed. She savored the ripple of sinew in the arms locked so tightly around the dip of her waist, the upper curve of her hips. His thighs were solid columns against her legs, and the bold hardness pressing into her abdomen proved that he was as aroused as she by the close contact between them.

He most definitely stayed in good shape. He slanted his mouth to a new angle against hers, his lips softening, hers parting. Tongues dipped, touched, teased. His hands slipped downward, while hers rose to wind around his neck, fingers sliding into his thick, slightly wavy hair.

Sensations ricocheted inside her. Her blood heated, coursed through her veins in increasingly turbulent waves. Her thoughts whirled, fragments of doubt, desire, fear and recklessness fighting for dominance.

She ached. Beneath her clothing, her skin tingled, needing more. The fingers of her right hand tightened in his hair while her left hand drifted downward to his shoulder, his warm, broad back. A low moan escaped her, and the sound seemed to galvanize him just as she'd thought he was pulling back. He lifted her against him, kissing her with a renewed fierceness that only fueled her own passion.

They made it to the bedroom only because the apartment was small. By the time they reached the bed, the hem of her dress was around her waist and Evan's shirt was mostly unbuttoned. She felt herself tumbling, felt the firmness of mattress against her back, the softness of pillow beneath her head. But she was aware of those things only peripherally. Her attention was on Evan, and the deliciously decadent things he was doing with her.

His hand was under her dress now, his work-roughened palm against the softest of her skin. Her body's reactions were familiar, and yet somehow all new. And it was amazing.

Her legs tangled with his. His mouth was at her throat, burrowing into the scoop of her neckline. He murmured something she didn't understand, but she didn't ask him to repeat it. She wasn't in the mood to talk just then.

Drawing his face to hers, she crushed whatever he might have said beneath her lips and surrendered herself to sensation.

Lingering in Evan's tidy bathroom, Renae checked her reflection in the big mirror over the sink. Her hair was neat, makeup freshened, dress straight and smoothed. She could return home confident that Lucy would never guess how she'd spent the past hour. At least, she hoped she would be able to keep her expression as unrevealing as her appearance.

As for the turmoil inside her, she'd have to deal with that later. When she was alone.

She couldn't say whether she regretted her actions, or whether she was likely to regret them. That, too, was something she would have to analyze in private.

She couldn't hide in here any longer, she told herself, stuffing her lipstick back into her bag. Drawing a deep breath, she made one last mirror check, then turned toward the door.

His own clothes rearranged, Evan waited in the living room, a glass of iced tea in his hand. He handed it to her, and she accepted it gratefully, taking a deep sip.

"I warmed the food," he said. "You can eat quickly before you head home, can't you?"

She didn't want to seem ungrateful for his efforts, but the thought of eating anything made her throat go tight. "I'm sorry, but I'm really not hungry."

"No problem. I'll put the leftovers in the fridge and have them for lunch tomorrow."

She nodded, relieved that he didn't press the issue. "The scholarship—"

"There really wasn't much left to do. I'll send you an email later with any final questions. There's no need for us to meet again until the applications arrive."

So it could be several weeks before she saw him again, and then Tate would probably be there, as well. She supposed that was for the best.

Leaning against the back of a chair, Evan studied her for a moment before saying, "You look ready to run."

"I'm not running," she corrected him somewhat primly. "I have things to do this evening. I'm sure you do, too."

"I've got time to talk for a few minutes, if you want."

"I, um—I'd better go."

She wasn't ready to talk about their lovemaking. Wasn't even ready to think about it too closely yet. She suspected she would spend many sleepless hours replaying every moment of it in her mind that night.

Again, he didn't push. "Okay. I'll talk to you later, then."

Would he call? She suspected he would. She'd take that call in her room, and hope Lucy would be none the wiser.

Turning toward the door, she hesitated when he said her name.

"Yes?" she asked without looking around.

"I'll be here at the same time next Wednesday, if you want to join me."

That made her head turn. She frowned at him in confusion. "Next Wednesday? I thought you said there was nothing more to do with the scholarship for now."

His gaze held hers. "There isn't."

She swallowed. "Oh."

He remained where he was, looking cool and casual as he continued to lounge against the chair, but Renae suspected he wasn't quite as relaxed as he appeared. She knew exactly what would happen if she came back next week. Just as she knew he knew.

"I'll…think about it," she said. And wasn't that an

understatement? She doubted she would think of anything else between now and then.

He nodded. Without giving him a chance to say anything else, she turned and let herself out of the apartment. Evan didn't try to detain her again.

Business cocktail parties were not Evan's idea of a good time. The fake smiles, the stilted conversation, the sizing up and kissing up—all of it was unappealing to his naturally straightforward personality. Still, he knew networking was part of owning a business, especially one that counted other businesses among its most lucrative clients. So, on Thursday evening, he stood in the moderately crowded, privately booked dining room of a trendy Little Rock restaurant, holding a drink he didn't want and swapping meaningless small talk with executives and clients of a prestigious architectural firm with whom he and Tate had contracted several jobs recently.

Across the room, Tate laughed at a joke told by the managing partner of a law firm that had recently announced plans to construct a new office building—which would, of course, need landscaping. Tate was better than Evan at mingling and glad-handing. Probably because he enjoyed it more.

"Evan Daugherty."

Suppressing a wince with an effort, he turned to face the sultry brunette who looked at him with her head cocked, her hands on her slender hips. "Hello, Ariel. How have you been?"

"Fortunately, not holding my breath waiting for you to call."

She had slipped him her number a couple months

earlier at another one of these gatherings. He'd stuffed it into his pocket and promptly forgotten about it.

He laughed lightly. "I sincerely doubt that you lack for calls."

"That's true," she conceded, preening a little. "But I still thought I would hear from you."

"Sorry, Ariel. I've been really busy lately. Work and winter planning, that sort of thing." Though he had no interest in going out with her, he didn't want to alienate her, either. Ariel was an account executive for the architectural firm.

She studied him through her thick lashes, obviously trying to gauge the extent of his interest in her. Or lack thereof. He kept his smile bland.

She tossed her head, making her long, glossy hair sway against her creamy shoulders, which were bared by the sleeveless midnight-blue top she wore with a tight gray pencil skirt. Evan assumed she had a jacket somewhere, since it was chilly outside on this early-November evening. For that matter, it wasn't exactly steamy here in the restaurant, but he wasn't surprised that Ariel would sacrifice comfort for sex appeal.

Tate appeared at his elbow, smiling flirtatiously. "Ariel. It's nice to see you here this evening."

She turned her attention to Evan's business partner. "Hello, Tate. How's marriage treating you?"

"It's great," he assured her. "We're very happy."

Evan noted that Tate didn't offer to pull out his phone-pictures for Ariel, probably because he was aware she wouldn't be at all interested in seeing them.

"That's nice," she said vaguely. "Though I never would have pegged you as the marrying type."

Tate laughed. "It surprised me, too."

"I'm beginning to wonder if your partner, here, has his eye on someone. He's got that look."

Evan raised an eyebrow. "That look?"

She patted his arm, her manicured fingers lingering a bit on his bicep. "Trust me. I've seen it before. You look to me like a man who's off the market."

He told himself not to read much into her words. Ariel would naturally look for any explanation for a man's lack of response to her come-ons. Still, Tate eyed him appraisingly before saying, "Yeah, I've been getting that feeling myself."

Ariel laughed musically. Apparently it was easy for her to handle a rebuff as long as she had a satisfactory explanation. And since she had always made it clear that she had no interest in tying herself down to any one man, she wouldn't compete for any guy who was looking for a long-term relationship.

Maybe he should have thought of that excuse before.

"You still have my number if it doesn't work out with the mystery woman," she said, flirting good-naturedly before drifting away.

He sighed in relief. "Thanks, Tate."

"For rescuing you? Not a problem. Not that you needed it. Ariel's just a compulsive flirt."

Evan glanced at his watch, wondering if it was too early to make an escape. Had he shaken hands and chatted with everyone he should?

"So, speaking of your mystery woman—how was Renae yesterday?" Tate asked, his tone a little too ingenuous.

Evan eyed him suspiciously. "She's fine."

"Hmm." Tate managed to convey quite a bit with that one syllable. Had he seen something in Evan's expression earlier?

Evan cleared his throat. "She's sending out the application packets next week. We'll all get together again around the middle of April to start looking through them."

"And when will you and Renae get together again?"

Evan frowned and set his unwanted drink on a nearby tray. "I don't know."

He still didn't exactly understand what had happened last time they'd been together. One minute they'd been standing across the room staring at each other, and the next they'd been tearing off each other's clothes. He really had planned to talk with her that evening, maybe clear the air of some old hurts and resentments— nothing more. He couldn't say he was sorry about what had taken place, instead— hell, it had been one of the more spectacular experiences of his adult life—but now he wasn't sure where they stood.

He hadn't planned to invite her to join him again next Wednesday. The words had just popped out of him as she was turning to leave. He didn't know if she would show up or, more likely, if she would talk herself out of it. As if he were somehow following the direction of Evan's thoughts, Tate nodded somberly.

"It's complicated," Evan said.

"I know."

Because this was neither the time nor place to discuss those complications, Evan turned toward the door. "I think we've been seen by everyone. I'm getting out of here."

"Hang on, I'll come with you. I told Kim I'd be home for dinner. You're welcome to join us, if you like."

Evan declined politely. He had a phone call he needed to make.

The children were in bed and Lucy was in the kitchen having a long telephone gossipfest with a friend from church when Evan's name popped up on Renae's phone that evening. Relieved that she didn't have to explain the call to anyone, she took it in her bedroom.

"How are you?" he asked.

There was no easy answer to that outwardly simple question, considering the emotional wringer she'd been through since she had left his apartment the evening before. She settled for a vague, "I'm fine, thank you. You?"

"Yeah, I'm good. And the kids? They're doing okay?"

"They're fine, too. They're in bed now."

"I thought they might be. I hope I'm not calling too late."

"No, it's okay. How was your day?" she asked for lack of anything else to say.

"I went to a networking thing—cocktails, small talk. Boring."

She couldn't imagine him enjoying that sort of gathering. "I'm sure it's a good way to keep your company name out there."

"Yeah, that's what Tate says. He's better at those things than I am, which is why I push him as the public face of our business. But I mentioned the scholarship to a few people and got some pledges for donations."

"That's great."

They chatted a few minutes longer about the party, the scholarship, her day at work, and then Evan said he was sure she had things to do. After they disconnected, Renae thought about how he had not mentioned what had happened between them yesterday, nor his invitation for next week.

He was giving her space, she decided. Subtly checking on her while making an effort not to pressure her. But somehow, even without directly referring to it, he'd left her thinking of their lovemaking, replaying it in her mind, aroused all over again—and for some reason, she thought he knew it.

She had stayed deliberately busy since she'd left him, telling herself she wasn't yet ready to analyze her impulsive actions, and certainly not ready to decide what she was going to do next week. Part of her—the sensible widowed mother and dutiful daughter-in-law part—ordered her to stop this now, before it spiraled out of control.

As if it hadn't already.

Another part of her—the young, healthy, single woman with natural needs and urges—ached to be with Evan again. It whispered temptingly at the back of her mind that she could have her cake and eat it, too—that she could keep her trysts with Evan separate from her "real life." That when she was with him, she could focus solely on the moment without worrying about the future or dwelling on the past. Was that crazy?

Lucy would certainly think so.

Groaning, she hid her face in her hands, calling herself every synonym for *idiot* she could remember spontaneously. If she had any sense at all, she would keep her distance from Evan.

If she wanted male companionship, she had other options. She could accept some of the matchmaking offers that had been directed her way. Or Mike Bishop was still available, and he was a nice guy. Good-looking. Nice kids. No past baggage between them, though he surely had scars from his divorce, even if it had seemed amicable enough to the outside observer.

Lucy might have a little trouble adjusting to Renae having an adult social life, but she would come around eventually. Especially if Renae went out with men who had no connection at all to the past.

The problem was, not one of the safe, relatively un-complicated men Renae had recently encountered made her heart race or her skin tingle just at the thought of him. Not one of them haunted her dreams or popped into her mind at the most inconvenient times during a busy day. And yet not one of them made her stomach knot with guilt and doubt and resentment and something that hovered all too closely to fear, either.

How foolish would she be to deliberately become entangled with the one man who made her feel all of those things?

Evan checked his watch for probably the third time in fifteen minutes. It was only five minutes past the time Renae had been showing up for their Wednesday meetings, but today those extra minutes seemed like an ominous sign.

He had told himself not to be surprised if she didn't show. He wasn't even expecting her, really, he assured himself. His invitation had hardly been smooth, certainly not romantic. Just, "I'll be here if you want to show up." He couldn't blame her for staying away, considering everything.

Even if it never happened again, he hoped Renae would remember the hour they had spent together last week without regrets or self-recrimination. They could tell themselves they had fulfilled some needs, satisfied an old curiosity. If that was the end of it, he hoped they could put their tangled feelings behind them and keep their future interactions pleasant. He would do everything he could to keep his own emotions deeply buried, leaving only the congenial old friend in place.

Releasing a sigh, he stood, turning toward the kitchen. He'd brought home Mexican takeout—he might as well eat. Maybe he would give Renae a friendly call later in the week, just to let her know he understood and that there were no hard feelings, though he probably wouldn't put it in so many words.

He froze when the buzzer sounded.

Swallowing hard, he crossed the room and pressed the release button. They could just talk, he assured himself. In fact, he wanted to talk with Renae. There was so much he didn't know about her life for the past seven years, so much he wanted to learn about her. They could have a real conversation that was not focused solely on the scholarship.

He opened the door to her, making an effort to keep his smile easy, to hide his surprise that she was there. Though she looked as beautiful as ever in a deep purple sweater and charcoal pants, her expression was somber and understandably wary.

Hoping to set her at ease, he closed the door behind her and motioned toward the kitchen. "I picked up chicken enchiladas. I hope you like Mexican food. Thought we could talk while we eat, if you want."

She smoothed her hands over the front of her pants, an unconsciously nervous gesture that revealed more than her expression. She turned then to face him. "I didn't come here to eat. Or to talk."

He could already feel his blood warming. He found the combination of vulnerability and defiance in her vivid blue eyes very appealing—but that was hardly a surprise, since nearly everything about Renae appealed to him.

He cleared his throat. "So why are you here?"

She spread her hands, her nose wrinkling in an endearing manner that sent his hot blood surging downward. "I think I came to tell you that I don't believe we should keep doing this."

Moving toward her, he kept his eyes on her face. "It's your call, of course."

"It's too complicated."

He nodded without stopping. "Yes."

She put up a hand when he reached her, but rather than hold him off, she rested her palm over his heart. She had to feel it banging against his chest. "It's irresponsible," she said.

"Maybe." He rested his hands on the upper curves of her hips.

"It doesn't mean anything. We're two young, healthy adults who happen to find each other attractive. That's all."

She seemed to stress the word *young*. Was she feeling her thirty years today? Would she believe him if he told her he thought she was absolutely stunning? That he wouldn't change a thing about her? Maybe his best bet was simply to show her.

He spoke with his mouth only a breath away from hers. "I can agree with that."

He brushed his lips against hers. Once, then again. Paused on the third pass to catch her lower lip just for a moment, then released it to press a full kiss on her mouth. He felt her fingers tighten on his chest, and then her arms were around his neck, her body flattened against his. Her lips parted, and he took advantage of the implied invitation, deepening the kiss with a thrust of his tongue.

He both heard and felt the soft moan that vibrated deep in her chest. He had never heard anything more arousing than the sounds Renae made when he kissed her, caressed her. He lifted her against him and she wrapped herself more snugly around him.

He didn't really want to talk just then, either.

"I can't find my right shoe. Do you see it?"

Fully dressed except for his own shoes, Evan sat on the bed, his back against the headboard, and watched as Renae wandered around the bedroom, still straightening her clothes as she searched for her other shoe. "Did you look under the bed?"

She dropped down to the floor and he admired the view as she peered under the edge of the comforter. "Not there."

"Maybe you left it in the living room." He swung his legs over the side and helped her to her feet, letting his hand linger just for a moment at the small of her back. He thought he'd be physically satisfied by now but the feel of her beneath his palm made his pulse rate trip.

Her cheeks seemed to go a shade pinker and he thought maybe he wasn't the only one reacting to the contact, but she moved away before he could be certain. Carrying her left shoe in her hand, she moved toward the doorway. "I'll go look. I can hardly go home wearing one shoe."

"Oh, I don't know. I think you look cute barefoot."

She looked over her shoulder at him, but she didn't smile. Swallowing, he followed her out of the room.

At the same time, they spotted the lone shoe lying in the short hallway just outside the bedroom. Renae pounced on it and quickly donned the pair. "Now, where did I leave my purse?"

"Food," he reminded her. "Enchiladas. All I have to do is pop them in the microwave."

She tucked one stray strand of blond hair behind her ear, drawing his attention to how sleek and tidy it looked despite their earlier activities. He was both impressed and a little daunted by how quickly and thoroughly she could hide any evidence of their lovemaking.

"Thanks, but I should go," she said without quite meeting his eyes. "I'll eat something later."

He caught her arm, stopping her restless movements and causing her to look up at him. "You've been here less than forty-five minutes. Surely you can take an extra few minutes to eat. Or are you running again?"

Her chin lifted a little and he could tell he'd piqued her pride—which, he had to admit to himself, had been his intention. "I'm not running."

"Are you afraid to sit down and talk with me for a few minutes?"

"Of course not. Why would I be afraid?"

Maybe she feared that he would make her face things she wasn't yet ready to acknowledge?

"I can't imagine," he said blandly. "Have a seat, Renae. I promise I won't keep you long."

She looked torn between escaping and staying to prove that she wasn't intimidated. He was gratified when she moved toward the table rather than the door. "Fine. I'll eat."

He knew better than to grin, but he did allow himself a small smile.

They were making progress.

Chapter Five

At the table, Evan made an effort to keep the conversation completely innocuous. "So, how long have you worked at the eye clinic?"

Still looking distracted, Renae stabbed her fork into the red-sauce-covered enchilada on her plate. "A little over a year. Since they opened."

"Dr. Sternberg seemed nice. Did a good job fitting my new contact lenses."

She nodded. "I like him, and his wife, Dr. Boshears. They're a very nice couple, good to work for."

"I mentioned to Dr. Sternberg that I knew you. I could tell he considers you a valuable member of the team."

She sipped her iced tea.

He searched for another topic that wouldn't edge too closely to the painful subjects they were both avoiding for now. "Got any big plans with the kids this weekend? The weather's supposed to be pretty much perfect for mid-November."

"We talked about going to the zoo Saturday, since it's supposed to be so pleasant. They love the zoo."

Asking about the kids seemed to be one way to get her to talk—he couldn't miss the way her eyes lit up when she spoke of them. "I never did see the Halloween photos you promised to show me."

Looking as though she wasn't sure he really wanted to see them, she punched a button on her phone and slid it toward him. He studied the screen, smiling at the two little superheroes posed dramatically in the photo. "Cute."

"Thanks."

The next photo was more of a close-up of the twins without their masks, huge grins on their faces as they showed off plastic pumpkins filled with candy. "This is their haul?"

"Yes. Our neighborhood really gets into Halloween."

"So I see. They must have had a great time."

"They did."

He glanced at the phone again before handing it back to her. He couldn't help feeling that Jason looked back at him from those fresh young faces. He didn't want to think about what Jason might say about Evan and Renae being together, even in this very tenuous way. Instead, he found himself wondering if he would ever meet his old friend's children.

Before he could figure out a way to ask, she set her fork on her plate, indicating she was finished eating. "What about you? Taking the bike out this weekend?

There should be some fall color left to admire Saturday."

He picked up his plate, stacked hers on top of it and moved toward the kitchen. "I sold my bike a week after the funeral. Haven't been on one since."

She sounded shocked when she said, "But you loved riding."

"I did." He wouldn't tell her now—maybe not ever—about the nightmares that had haunted him for so long after that last ride.

She sat silently behind him, processing his admission.

Rejoining her, he said lightly, "I still like rides in the country on a rare free afternoon. I just take my truck now."

This would probably be the time to talk about the accident. About the grief and regret he'd felt afterward, and what he would give to go back and change the events of that day. Yes, it was complicated, considering his feelings for Renae. Like most men, he tended to avoid deep, emotion-based discussions—but maybe it would be good for them to get those things out in the open.

"I really do have to get home," Renae said, rising to her feet.

Now she really was running, he figured. From the memories their mention of the motorcycle had stirred. From the conversation that was becoming more inevitable every time they were together—and which they both dreaded for reasons of their own.

Though they had said little of substance while they'd eaten, he was glad that they had at least taken that small amount of time for conversation. He wanted to make it clear that sex wasn't the only reason he had invited her to join him today—though he wouldn't blame her for doubting that, since they seemed to fall into each other's arms now every time they were alone together.

On an impulse, he said, "Maybe next week we could meet at a restaurant? You know, for a nice meal?"

It must have been too much, and maybe too soon after the oblique reference to Jason's accident. He could almost see Renae draw back even further. "I, uh—"

"Or we could meet here again," he said smoothly.

Renae ran a hand over her hair though it was already immaculate. She looked at him gravely, all vulnerability hidden now, her expression hard to read. "I don't know what we're doing here, exactly. But I do know we're playing with fire."

He shook his head. "I'm not playing."

Like her, he didn't know exactly what was happening between them. Where it might lead, other than to more regrets. But he wanted to make it very clear he wasn't toying with her. That he was as much a prisoner to this magnetism between them as she seemed to be. Maybe just as much an unwilling captive.

He hadn't been looking for an entanglement with anyone—certainly not a woman who came with as many obstacles as Renae. The past. Her kids. Her mother-in-law. He'd be crazy to even think about getting mixed up with her in more than this superficially physical way.

And yet he heard himself saying, "I'll be here next week."

She blinked, then lifted her chin and moved toward the door. Was she not even going to say good-night?

He caught her arm to stop her. She looked composed

and confident, but when he studied her eyes, he saw just how misleading that impression was. Sighing a little, he brushed a kiss over her mouth.

"Just think about it," he said when he released her and stepped away.

She nodded and let herself out without speaking, leaving him to wonder once more if he would see her again.

And why he wanted so badly to do so, considering the pain she had caused him in the past.

In response to an emailed request from Tate, Renae flipped through an old photo album Thursday evening looking for an appealing shot of Jason to use on the scholarship website. They didn't want a formal, posed photograph, but something casual, laughing— something very representative of Jason.

She chose a snapshot she had taken of him only a few months before his death. In it, he stood on a boulder at the top of Petit Jean Mountain on a clear summer day with blue sky above him and the green-and-blue Arkansas River Valley spread behind him. A breeze tossed his dark hair and his polished-ebony eyes had sparkled with amusement and energy. The shot had captured Jason perfectly. She had the photo stored in her computer, so it would work well for the website.

Leslie sat on the living room floor, looking through another old album. Lucy was on the couch with her knitting and Daniel played with an elaborate building-blocks set while Boomer snored on the hearth of the small, gas-flame fireplace. It had been a rare, quiet evening at home, the type Renae usually savored. She was enjoying it now, but would find it even more relaxing if she could just keep random thoughts of Evan from popping erratically into her head.

"Who are these people, Mama?"

Pushing her worries about Evan to the back of her mind, Renae motioned to her daughter. "Let me see."

Leslie set the album in Renae's lap, then leaned over the arm of the chair to point. "That's you. And that's Daddy."

"Yes, that's right." The twins had seen many photographs of the father they'd never met, and had been told many stories about him. Both Renae and Lucy wanted them to feel that they knew him as much as possible.

Leslie pointed to another photo. "Who is this girl?"

"That's my friend Jeannie. She moved to Colorado when you were just a baby."

Turning the page, Leslie asked, "Who are these guys?"

"Um…" Renae cleared her throat, looking at the photo of three young men posing humorously for the camera, laughing and looking happy just to be hanging out together. "That's your daddy, of course. And those are his friends Tate and Evan."

From the couch, Lucy made a disgruntled sound. It made Renae think of Evan's question about whether Lucy spat on the ground when she heard his name.

"Daddy's friends look nice," Leslie said.

"They're the men who are making a scholarship in your daddy's name," Renae said evenly. "They'll give money to boys who want to go to college but can't afford it."

"Only boys?" Leslie asked with a frown.

"There are other scholarships for girls, but this one is for boys."

"Because Daddy was a boy. Duh," Daniel said without looking up from the robot he was building with little red-and-blue-plastic snap-together blocks.

Renae smiled, but she noted that Lucy did not. Even one of Daniel's cute comments couldn't lighten Lucy's mood, caused by just hearing Evan's name.

Now was definitely not the time to mention that she'd been seeing Evan on a regular basis. And that she was strongly tempted to continue doing so.

Swallowing a sigh, Renae closed the album. "I'm going to put these away now," she said. "You and Daniel need to get ready for bed. Who's taking the first bath?"

"She is."

"He is."

"It's Daniel's turn to go first," Lucy said from the couch.

Daniel sighed gustily. "Can Boomer take a bath with me?"

"No." It was the same answer Renae always gave when he asked that question, but it was practically a tradition now for him to ask. "Hurry up, it's getting late."

Throwing his building toys into the box, he carried the set with him as he left the room, dragging his feet a little just to make a statement.

Chuckling, Renae gathered the albums and stood to return them to her room. Her cell phone chimed before she'd made it through the doorway. Aware of Lucy's sharp look, she kept walking. She would take the call in private. It might not be Evan, of course—she did have other friends who called to chat occasionally— but something told her whose name she would see on her phone.

"Hi," Evan said when she answered. "Bad time?"

"I'm about to put the kids to bed, but I have a couple of minutes."

"That's all I need. I called to tell you about something that came up today during lunch with Tate and some of our friends. Just to run it past you."

"Oh? What is it?"

"Tate's wife and his sister both work with Emma Grainger, who's an occupational therapist. We all have lunch together on Wednesdays. Anyway, Emma's family hosts a big holiday party every December and they always take up a collection for charity at the event, to be split between several of the family's pet causes. This year, Emma wants to add our scholarship to the mix. Lynette had the idea of having a silent auction at the party with donated items. Emma talked to her parents and they're on board, so she just called to tell me about it."

"That's very nice of her and her family. Do they have time to pull it all together?"

"Emma says yes. She's doing it rather casually, so she warned that it could just be a small donation, but I told her we'd take anything we could get."

"Of course. Gratefully. What sort of items will they be auctioning?"

"Pretty much anything. Tate and I are donating a couple of potted patio trees."

"Good idea. I'll ask Ann and Gary if they want to make a donation. Last year they gave a nice pair of sunglasses to Cathy for a fundraiser for her kids' school."

"Yeah, that would be great. They'd be credited for the donation, of course."

She thought of the beautifully knitted afghans and

baby blankets Lucy made endlessly for charities. "Do you think a hand-knit afghan would auction well?"

"Sure, especially this time of year. Why, do you knit?"

"I don't, but Lucy does. She makes gorgeous lap blankets for her church and the hospital auxiliary. I bet she'd provide one for the auction." Maybe Lucy would feel more connected to the cause if she made a personal contribution.

"Even if she knows I'm involved?"

His voice had cooled significantly with the mention of Lucy. She couldn't entirely blame him. "I'm sure Lucy would love to make a donation to the scholarship in Jason's name," she said in defense of her mother-in-law.

At least, she hoped Evan's involvement wasn't enough to turn Lucy against their charity. Lucy did hold strong resentment against Evan. Renae didn't entirely blame her, either—which put her squarely in the middle between the two.

No, not in the middle, she corrected herself quickly. She was on Lucy's side, of course. Lucy was her family, her mother in every way but biology. She didn't know what she'd have done without Lucy when the twins were born, and in the years since. Maybe Lucy wasn't being entirely fair to Evan, but Lucy had lost her child, and she dealt with that loss as best she could.

It would be best just to keep Lucy and Evan apart.

"I'd better go," she said. "It's bath time and bedtime for the twins."

"I understand. Just one more thing. Emma has invited all of us to the party. It's the first Saturday in December, if you want to check your calendar."

"Oh, I—"

"You could come with Tate and Kim and Lynette and me to represent the scholarship fund," he added casually. "Just in case anyone at the party has any questions or wants faces to put with the request."

The way he put it made her reluctant to say no. As if she would be slacking on her part in the effort if she didn't make an appearance. At least he wasn't making it sound like a date with him, but a gathering with everyone who had any interest in the scholarship. She would have to be very careful explaining it to Lucy, but she saw no real harm in representing Jason at the fundraiser. "All right. I'll try to be there."

"Great. Maybe you'd like to join us for lunch one Wednesday so you can meet everyone involved beforehand. We get together at a Chinese place in Little Rock for a quick meal, since everyone has to get back to work afterward and the girls only have an hour free."

Even more time in Evan's company. This was getting more and more complicated. "I'll think about it."

"Okay, I'll let you go. You know how to reach me if you need anything."

"Yes."

"And you know where I'll be Wednesday evening," he added somberly.

She swallowed hard. "Good night, Evan."

"Sleep well."

As if that would happen, she thought, disconnecting the call. She hadn't slept completely well since Evan Daugherty had come back into her life.

She waited until the twins were in bed before talking with Lucy. They were in the kitchen, Lucy at the table with a mug of chamomile tea while Renae prepared the next day's lunches for herself and the kids. Zipping carrot sticks into snack-sized plastic bags, Renae asked with studied casualness, "Lucy, do you have an extra lap quilt for a charity donation?"

"I have that pretty white one I finished last week. I was very pleased with the way that one turned out. I thought I might send it as a door prize for the church holiday crafts fair, but I've already got a couple ready for them, so I could let you have it if you need it. What's the charity?"

Renae glanced over her shoulder. "It's a fundraiser auction for the Jason Sanchez Memorial Scholarship."

Lucy's mouth quivered. "I see."

"A blanket made by Jason's mother would be a special contribution, I think. Very meaningful for whoever buys it."

"Who's running this auction?"

"A local family named Grainger. They throw a holiday party every December and it's their practice to raise money for charities at the event. They're adding the scholarship to this year's list, which is very generous of them, I think."

Lucy blinked a couple of times, and Renae could tell she was a bit surprised. She had probably expected to hear Evan's name. "I don't know these Graingers. Were they friends of yours and Jason's?"

"No. Their daughter, Emma, works with Tate's sister. Emma heard about the scholarship and thought it was a worthy cause."

Lucy looked torn, and Renae thought it was easy enough to understand why. Naturally, Lucy wanted the scholarship to succeed, but she still hated that Evan and Tate were the ones who had started it. Especially Evan.

"I'll donate the blanket," Lucy said after a moment, picking up her teacup again. "To the Grainger family, for my Jason's scholarship."

"I'm sure they'll be pleased."

Lucy sighed. "Jason would have loved this scholarship."

"Yes, he would have." Stashing the lunches in the fridge, Renae rested a hand on Lucy's plump shoulder. "It's the perfect way to honor his memory."

Lucy reached up to cover Renae's hand with her own. "It is. Even if it was started to soothe Evan Daugherty's guilty conscience," she grumbled.

Leaning over to brush a kiss against Lucy's soft cheek, Renae gave a little chuckle. "Whatever the reason, it's a good thing. Thank you for donating the blanket."

"I love you, Renae."

Swallowing a lump in her throat, Renae held on to her smile with an effort. "Love you, too. Good night, Lucy."

The next week was hectic at the clinic. With the holidays coming up soon, patients were trying to get their eye exams in beforehand. Those with vision-coverage insurance plans needed appointments before the end of the year, and many had put off scheduling until the last minute.

Renae stayed so busy she barely had time to look at the clock Wednesday afternoon, though she was aware of the passing minutes. She told herself it was just as well she was occupied. She would just stay a little later than usual, then head home.

She didn't need to see Evan today. It would be better if she didn't. Even if every inch of her ached to be with him. Which only made her more certain she should stay away.

Taking advantage of a brief lull, her coworker Cathy glanced at the clock at 5:45. "Today's your scholarship meeting, isn't it, Renae?"

"Oh, I can skip it today," Renae said airily, keeping her eyes focused on some papers in front of her. "As busy as we are, I should stay a little late to help."

"No need for that. The last patients are in with the doctors now, so Lisa and I can handle everything."

"But—"

"Seriously, Renae. Go to your meeting. We've all noticed how much you're enjoying them."

"I, uh— What?"

Cathy smiled. "You just always seem to look forward to them. I can't blame you. That good-looking guy who came in to see Dr. Sternberg a few weeks ago is on the committee, right?"

"Yes, he's one of the scholarship founders," Renae agreed vaguely.

"But you have to admit he is also seriously hot."

"Smoking hot," Lisa agreed soberly from her nearby desk. Until then, Renae hadn't even realized Lisa was listening.

Renae shook her head. "You two are incorrigible."

Cathy snorted. "Like you don't agree with us. You think we haven't noticed how nicely you've been dressing lately? Even on days other than Wednesdays. It's like you've suddenly started paying a little more attention to your clothes and makeup—which is a good thing."

Renae was a little taken aback. Maybe she had been

dressing with a bit more care lately—not that she'd been exactly sloppy before, she thought with a frown. She'd simply tried to be a bit more fashionable, more age-appropriate, not falling into the sort of matronly rut Lucy favored. She'd thought the changes were subtle, that her coworkers wouldn't even notice. Apparently, they were more observant than she'd given them credit for.

"You look nice," Lisa agreed, nodding.

Cathy pointed a finger meaningfully toward Renae. "Wouldn't hurt you to go out with a smoking-hot guy. You're young and single, the kids are getting old enough to be more self-sufficient. And by the way, find out if he has a brother, will you?"

"He doesn't. He has a sister," Renae replied without thinking.

Cathy looked rather pleased, as if there were some significance to the personal knowledge. Lisa giggled.

Exasperated with both of them, Renae slid a patient file into place. When she turned, she found Cathy standing behind her, holding Renae's purse.

"Go to your meeting," Cathy said. "We'll see you in the morning."

"Go," Lisa echoed. "You deserve to have a little fun."

"I don't know what they're talking about," Ann said, sticking her head through the doorway with a grin, "but sounds to me like you should go, Renae."

"See? It's unanimous," Cathy laughed. "Even your boss is ordering you to go."

Releasing a sigh, Renae plucked her purse from Cathy's hands. "Fine. I'll go. I'll see you all tomorrow."

Who was she to argue when everyone in her office thought she should go?

* * *

Evan was almost smiling when he opened his door to her a short time later. "It's always a surprise when you show up," he admitted in lieu of greeting.

She poked him with a finger, pushing him backward a couple steps. "It wasn't my idea for me to come here tonight," she informed him.

Something about her recklessly challenging tone seemed to startle him. "It wasn't?"

She tossed her bag on a chair. "No."

"Then, um, whose idea was it?"

"Apparently it was unanimous." Advancing toward him, she placed her hands on his shoulders, her eyes narrowed on his face. "Everyone at work seems to think I need to, um, have fun, as they so delicately phrased it."

His mouth twitched with a grin he must have known better than to release just then. "And are you having fun now?"

She started unfastening the buttons of his blue shirt. "I'm about to be."

His hands settled on the curves of her hips. He cleared his throat, but his voice was still husky when he said, "I thought maybe we could talk some this evening."

"Talking is not fun." She spread his shirt and let her hands wander across his broad, sleek chest. His skin was so warm. She could already imagine it against her own, and the image took her breath away.

She rose on tiptoes and caught his lower lip between her teeth for a light nip. "Are you sure you want to talk?" she murmured against his mouth.

A distant part of her mind marveled at her behavior. This wasn't like her—or hadn't been like her for a very long time. Flirtatious, seductive, a little mischievous. It was a part of herself she had put away years ago. Who'd have thought Evan Daugherty would bring it out again?

He hesitated only a moment, until she wrapped her arms around his neck and pressed herself more snugly against him. A low groan escaped him then, a sound she found immensely satisfying. He reached down, swept an arm behind her knees and lifted her into his arms. She laughed and clutched at his shoulders in surprise and pleasure.

She hadn't seen Evan's playful side in the past few weeks, either. The man she was getting to know now was much more serious and pensive than the footloose young man she had known so briefly before.

Time and experience had changed them both—but still they were drawn together. The guy was still a walking heartache, she had no doubt of that. She wouldn't let herself mistake lust and infatuation for anything more lasting or life-altering. But for tonight, at least, she would take advantage of this rare hour or so away from her responsibilities and…well, have fun. Just as her coworkers had advised her.

Evan dropped her on his bed, and she landed with a bounce and a breathless laugh. Reaching up, she caught his open shirt and pulled him down on top of her. Shoes landed on the floor beside the bed with muffled thumps. Their mouths fused in deep, hungry kisses. They fumbled with zippers and hems and pushed fabric away to reveal flushed, dampening skin. Legs tangled, hands roamed and grasped, mouths sought, explored, tasted. Renae arched off the bed with a gasp when Evan tugged an aching nipple lightly between his teeth, then soothed it with a leisurely stroke of his tongue.

Her hands tangled in his hair, fingers tightening when he nibbled his way down her body. His fingers dug lightly into her upper thighs, bending her knee and lifting her leg around him. She bowed off the mattress with a strangled cry when he took another little nip, and heard him laugh roughly in response.

Spurred into competition, she tugged at him, pushed at him until he lay on his back beside her and she could loom over him. She nipped at his jaw, stroked a fingertip slowly down his body from his sternum to circle his shallow navel, then traced a line even lower. Now it was Evan who squirmed and moaned, and she who laughed breathlessly…until he silenced that laughter with a coherence-shattering kiss.

By the time he donned protection and thrust into her, playfulness had changed to burning, almost-desperate need. They found that satisfaction together, their soft cries harmonizing perfectly in the darkening bedroom.

Chapter Six

"Well?"

Renae drew a long, deep breath, settling her pulse rate before she spoke. "Well, what?"

"Was it fun?"

She was surprised into a quick laugh. "Yes, I suppose it was."

Propped on one arm beside her in his bed, Evan reached out to stroke a strand of hair from her cheek. "Going to tell your coworkers you took their advice?"

Her laugh changed to a rueful grimace. "Not exactly."

"Just curious."

She started to turn her head toward the nightstand, but he caught her jaw to prevent her from doing so. "Don't check the clock yet. You still have some time."

"I do have to get home soon," she reminded him. "Lucy will worry if I'm late."

A frown flickered over his face at the mention of Lucy's name. Renae now expected him and Lucy to scowl at any mention of the other, which was rather annoying.

"You and Lucy have no plans to set up separate households again anytime soon?" he asked, his tone a bit too casual.

"We've never discussed it."

"I understand why she moved in to help with the twins when they were babies, but now that they're older, it seems like you'd both want your own places. I mean, how old is Lucy—sixty, sixty-one?"

"She's fifty-nine."

"Even younger than I thought. She was young when the twins were born—still is, really. Doesn't she want a social life of her own? Don't you?"

"We've had a good life," Renae said, hearing a note of defensiveness in her voice. "Those first couple of years were tough, of course, and we stayed incredibly busy with the babies. Daniel had some health problems as a newborn, and he needed a lot of care. By the time things settled down, we'd gotten into a comfortable routine. Lucy has her friends and activities at church. I have my friends, and my Wednesday evenings on my own. It works for us."

He shook his head. "Just seems like it would feel like living with your mother at thirty."

"I suppose it does," she said softly. "I barely remember living with my mother, but Lucy has been like a mom to me almost since we met. We disagree sometimes, but for the most part we get along amazingly well."

"That's great, I guess," he said, hardly convinced,

"but it still seems like having her there would limit your social activities."

She shrugged. "My activities are more limited by my six-year-old twins than by my mother-in-law."

He thought about that for a moment. "I can see that," he acknowledged. "Even if Lucy didn't live with you, I doubt you'd want to bring a man home after a date when you've got young kids in the house."

"It hasn't really been an issue. There haven't been many dates, and there was no one I wanted to bring home afterward."

Realizing it was a very strange conversation to be having at that particular time—not to mention while lying naked in Evan's bed—she rolled to look at the clock despite his earlier objection. He was right, she did have a little time yet. But now she was self-conscious.

Evan was still focused on her social life, for some reason. "Does Lucy object to you dating?"

"Of course not." Perhaps she'd spoken with a bit more force than necessary, but she assured herself it was the truth. Maybe Lucy wasn't enthusiastic about Renae dating, but she had never actually objected.

"And if she knew you were here with me? What would she say?"

Renae couldn't quite suppress her grimace. "I think you already know the answer to that, Evan."

His face was suddenly grim. "Yeah, I guess I do."

She didn't understand why Evan kept pushing the subject of Lucy's antipathy toward him. He knew very well how Lucy felt, and he should understand why, even if he didn't agree with her. And he had to know that Renae's loyalties lay with the woman who had been such a vital part of her little family for all these years.

It wasn't as if he and she were seriously involved anyway. She didn't know exactly what they *were* doing, but she figured the fire would burn out soon enough.

She reached for Evan's discarded shirt, wrapping it around herself as she slid out of the bed. Evan didn't try to detain her, but she felt him watching her as she gathered her clothes and padded toward the bathroom.

Evan must have ducked into the half bathroom while Renae dressed. She could smell food when she walked out of his bedroom, leaving his shirt folded on the end of the bed. He was always feeding her—it was rather sweet of him, actually.

This time Evan hadn't stopped for takeout. Renae's eyes widened when she saw the table. "You cooked?"

Evan looked a little sheepish. "I got home early this afternoon. Had a little extra time. It's just spaghetti with meat sauce and garlic bread. Nothing fancy."

"You shouldn't have gone to the trouble."

He shrugged. "I didn't even know for sure you'd be here but I figured it was worth a shot."

Had he really not expected her? Was he so oblivious to how strongly she was drawn to him, no matter how hard she fought it?

They chatted about inconsequential things during the meal, avoiding mention of anything important. Evan talked about his work, about some of the plans he and Tate had for expanding their business, and she saw the ambition in his eyes. She had no doubt that they would soon be one of the premier landscape design firms in the state. She asked a lot of questions, and the time passed so quickly she had to hurriedly finish her meal when she glanced at her watch.

"We didn't talk about the scholarship tonight," Evan

said as they cleared the table. "We should probably look things over next week, make sure we're still on track for the coming semester."

Though he'd just said he wasn't sure she'd come this evening, he seemed to be taking for granted now that she would be back next week. Thinking of her calendar, she shook her head. "I won't be here next week."

Evan went still. A frown cut a line between his dark brows. "You won't?"

She could see that her words had taken him aback. Maybe he thought she was breaking it off with him. She probably should, before everything got even more complicated between them than it already was.

"Next Wednesday is the night before Thanksgiving. I'll have too much to do getting ready for the holiday."

His expression cleared and she thought she saw some of the tension leave his shoulders. "Oh. Yeah, I forgot about the holiday."

She would think later about how dismayed he'd seemed before her clarification—and what that meant about this no-strings, purely physical affair she'd thought they were having. She said the first thing that came to mind to distract herself as she gathered her things to leave. "Do you have plans for Thanksgiving?"

He nodded. "My grandparents in Batesville are hosting the family. My sister's coming from St. Louis, and our parents are flying in from San Diego."

She remembered that he had grown up in Little Rock, but his parents had relocated to San Diego because of his dad's career when Evan was in college. At loose ends on weekends after that, Evan had spent time hanging out with Jason and Tate, occasionally getting into mild mischief, from what Renae had gleaned later from

Jason and Lucy. That had been a couple years before she'd met Jason, but she had no trouble picturing the three friends raising a little hell during their college years. Lucy might have tried to cast Evan in the role of ringleader, but Renae had no doubt that Jason had contributed his share of ideas.

"I'm sure you'll enjoy visiting with your family."

"Lots of food and football," he replied lightly. "What's not to enjoy?"

She smiled. "Lucy and I are cooking a traditional Thanksgiving meal. A couple of widowed neighbors are joining us for lunch, since neither of them have family to share the holidays with."

He managed not to frown this time in response to the mention of her mother-in-law. She supposed that was progress. "That's generous of you," he said.

"They're both very sweet ladies. We enjoy spending time with them."

Crossing his arms over his chest, Evan leaned against the back of the couch. She sensed a lingering tension in him she couldn't quite explain.

"What about your family?" he asked. "Will you see any of them for the holiday?"

She toyed with the strap of her bag. His question only highlighted how little they really knew each other. "My father died last year. My few remaining relatives have scattered, and I don't see them very often now."

He grimaced. "I'm sorry. I didn't know about your dad."

"It's okay."

She wasn't sure how much Evan remembered—or had ever known—about her rootless past. She had been very young when her mother died of an allergic reaction to a medication. Her father, a truck driver who had spent more time on the road than at home, had left his young daughter to be passed around among a couple of aunts with whom she had never bonded. Her childhood hadn't been an unhappy one, exactly, but she had definitely been vulnerable when she'd met naturally demonstrative Jason and his inherently nurturing mother—lonely, and hungry for affection and stability.

"Well," she said, shoving those thoughts to the back of her mind. "I'd better go. It's getting late."

Pushing away from the couch, Evan walked with her to the door. "Enjoy your Thanksgiving, Renae."

She smiled up at him. "Thank you. You, too."

He lowered his head to kiss her. The kiss was long, slow and so thorough that her head wasn't quite clear by the time he finally, reluctantly, released her.

"I'll call you," he said.

She swallowed hard, trying to steady her voice before she replied. "The kids are always in bed by nine. Any time after that is good."

"I'll keep that in mind."

He kissed her again. Feeling her knees start to weaken, she gave him a light push, putting distance between them before she was tempted to stay awhile longer. "Good night, Evan."

She was out the door before he had a chance to respond. Standing in the hallway outside his apartment, she rested her hand on the wall, needing a moment to collect herself before heading for her car. She didn't hear Evan moving inside. Either the door muffled sounds, or he was still standing where she had left him.

They were separated by only a few feet and a couple inches of wood, but the distance between them seemed so much farther. Whatever drew them together—attraction, chemistry, whatever it could be called—it was not enough to overcome all the issues that kept them apart. The attraction had been there nine years ago, too, but all it had brought her was heartache, guilt and confusion.

As she walked to the car, she assured herself she wouldn't risk everything she had accomplished during the past seven years just because sexy Evan Daugherty had strolled back into her life.

The blessing Lucy gave over their bountiful Thanksgiving dinner expressed gratitude for the food, for their home and their health, for the two dear friends who had joined them that day, and for all their happy memories of loved ones no longer with them. By the time she said "amen," the adults gathered around the dining room table were all damp-eyed.

Fortunately, the children brightened the moment with their holiday delight.

"I want lots of sweet potatoes," Leslie said, bouncing in her chair. "With extra marshmallow topping."

"You'll have plenty of sweet potatoes," Renae assured her daughter with a smile. "But you need to eat some of the other dishes, too. Mrs. Whelan's green beans smell delicious, and I'm sure you'll like the dressing Mrs. Sinclair made to go with Grammy's beautiful turkey."

Daisy and Maxine beamed in response to Renae's compliments about the dishes they had contributed. Daisy's son would be home for Christmas, but couldn't make both holidays, leaving the widowed sisters at loose ends for Thanksgiving. Renae was sure they'd had other invitations, and she was pleased that they'd chosen to celebrate with her family. The twins loved having guests.

"Be sure and save room for dessert," Daisy urged the children. "I made chocolate pie and Maxine brought pumpkin pie. And I think I saw that your grandma made a coconut pie and sugar cookies."

The twins squirmed eagerly in their chairs. Renae swallowed a sigh, thinking of the sugar highs ahead.

The adults lingered at the table with cups of tea after dessert as the children dashed outside to work off some of their excess energy. The weather was cool but pleasant, requiring only jackets to keep them comfortable as they ripped around the fenced backyard with the growing pup who'd been banished outside for the day.

"Your children are so well behaved, Renae," Daisy said approvingly, glancing through the glass door that led out to the backyard. "You've taught them excellent table manners for such a young age."

"Thank you," Renae replied, pleased. "But I have to give a lot of the credit to Lucy. She is such a help to me with the twins."

Lucy beamed.

Maxine glanced from Lucy to Renae. "It's so nice that you two get along so well. I never could have lived with my mother-in-law. There'd have been all-out war in the household if we'd tried. Mean old biddy," she added in a wry undertone. "Rest her soul."

Renae swallowed a laugh. "I lucked out when it came to my mother-in-law. I couldn't have asked for a better one."

Lucy blinked rapidly. "I feel the same way about my daughter-in-law."

"So nice," Daisy said. "You two have made a lovely home here for the children."

Lucy's smile faded. She glanced at one of the empty chairs at the table. "We've done our best."

Having suffered losses of their own, the other women nodded understandingly. When a spate of happy barking followed by a chorus of giggles drifted in through the glass door, they all smiled.

Lucy shook her head. "That dog is a handful. I thought Renae had lost her mind when she agreed to let them bring him home. But I have to admit, the twins love him dearly and they do take good care of him."

A ball flew past the door, followed by the dog and then the kids racing him toward the prize.

Maxine chuckled. "Must be nice to be so young and have that much energy after such a big meal while the older folk sit here getting sleepy."

Once again her senior citizen neighbor was treating Renae as a chronological peer. It didn't shake her as badly today as it had on Halloween. Maybe because she was more accustomed to hearing it now. Or maybe because she'd been feeling younger and more desirable lately—and she knew exactly who to thank for that.

Even if she and Evan were never alone together again, she would be grateful to him for making her feel attractive again, she thought somewhat wistfully. She was hardly going to hit up the singles bars or sign up for a matchmaking service after she and Evan went their own ways again, but still, it was nice to feel this way, if only for a little while.

"So, Evan. Are you seeing anyone?"

Swallowing a bite of gooey pecan pie, he washed it

down with a sip of coffee before replying deliberately vaguely to his grandmother's question. "I've been really busy with the business lately, Mimi. We're just slowing down a little for winter, but summer was crazy."

"That's a good thing, isn't it?" his dad asked.

"You bet. Tate and I have been pleased with our growth this year."

"And what about the book?" his mother inquired. "How's that coming along?"

He and Tate had been working on a photo-essay book about urban gardening, collaborating with a young local photographer who'd shot some of their most successful and impressive projects during the summer. "We haven't made much progress, but we're hoping to put some time into it after the first of the year, before the spring gardening rush starts again."

"And the scholarship?" his sister, Caroline, asked, joining in the inquisition. "How's that going?"

He took another bracing sip of coffee. "Very well. Renae Sanchez has been working with us to nail down all the details before we start accepting applications for next year."

Caroline eyed him narrowly while the others got sidetracked with a discussion about which of their friends could be counted on to contribute to the scholarship fund. Three years his senior, Caroline was the one member of his family who would best understand his mixed feelings about working so closely with Renae.

Caroline had been the one he'd gone to the night of Jason's funeral, and to whom he had poured out his grief, his survivor's guilt, his dismay that Lucy placed so much blame on him. And his hurt that Renae had said nothing in his defense when Lucy all but accused him at the funeral of causing Jason's death. He had looked at Renae, hoping for support, or at least a sign that she didn't agree. Instead, she had put an arm around Lucy's shoulders, turned and led her away without looking back at Evan.

Reading between the lines of his outpouring of words, his sister had asked him that night if he was in love with Renae.

"Maybe I could have been," he had answered her after a long, choked pause. "But she loved Jason."

"And so did you," Caroline had said, placing a hand on her brother's cheek.

Covering her hand with his, he had struggled against tears. It had been the last time he'd cried—for Jason, and for himself.

Caroline caught him alone a short while after Thanksgiving dinner, while the various other members of the family mingled elsewhere in their grandparents' home. "So, you've been working with Renae Sanchez."

He nodded, glancing around to make sure no one else could overhear. "We meet once a week to, uh, talk about the scholarship."

As close as he was to his sister, he wouldn't tell her everything that had gone on between himself and Renae during the past few weeks. Maybe he had his flaws, but he still tried to be a gentleman.

Snugly zipped into a fitted coat, with a pretty scarf wrapped around her throat, his brown-haired, brown-eyed sister reached out absently to pluck a shriveled leaf from a bush in their grandmother's garden. "It's been—what?—six years since Jason died?"

"Seven." Sometimes it felt like yesterday, he mused, staring at a bubbling concrete fountain without really

Send For
2 FREE BOOKS
Today!

I accept your offer!

Please send me two free
Harlequin® Special Edition®
novels and two mystery
gifts (gifts worth about $10).
I understand that these books
are completely free—even
the shipping and handling will
be paid—and I am under no
obligation to purchase anything, ever,
as explained on the back of this card.

235/335 HDL FEHN

Please Print

FIRST NAME

LAST NAME

ADDRESS

APT.#   CITY

STATE/PROV.   ZIP/POSTAL CODE

Visit us online at
www.ReaderService.com

The Reader Service—Here's how it works: Accepting your 2 free books and 2 free gifts (gifts valued at approximately $10.00) places you under no obligation to buy anything. You may keep the books and gifts and return the shipping statement marked "cancel". If you do not cancel, about a month later we'll send you 6 additional books and bill you just $4.49 each in the U.S. or $5.24 each in Canada. That is a savings of at least 14% off the cover price. It's quite a bargain! Shipping and handling is just 50¢ per book in the U.S. or 75¢ per book in Canada.* You may cancel at any time, but if you choose to continue, every month we'll send you 6 more books, which you may either purchase at the discount price or return to us and cancel your subscription.

*Terms and prices subject to change without notice. Prices do not include applicable taxes. Sales tax applicable in N.Y. Canadian residents will be charged applicable taxes. Offer not valid in Quebec. Credit or debit balances in a customer's account(s) may be offset by any other outstanding balance owed by or to the customer. Please allow 4 to 6 weeks for delivery. Offer available while quantities last. All orders subject to credit approval. Books received may not be as shown.

▼ If offer card is missing write to: The Reader Service, P.O. Box 1867, Buffalo, NY 14240-1867 or visit www.ReaderService.com ▼

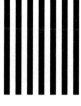

NO POSTAGE
NECESSARY
IF MAILED
IN THE
UNITED STATES

BUSINESS REPLY MAIL
FIRST-CLASS MAIL   PERMIT NO. 717   BUFFALO, NY

POSTAGE WILL BE PAID BY ADDRESSEE

THE READER SERVICE
PO BOX 1867
BUFFALO NY 14240-9952

Send For
2 FREE BOOKS
Today!

I accept your offer!

Please send me two free
Harlequin® Special Edition®
novels and two mystery
gifts (gifts worth about $10).
I understand that these books
are completely free—even
the shipping and handling will
be paid—and I am under no
obligation to purchase anything, ever,
as explained on the back of this card.

235/335 HDL FEHN

Please Print

FIRST NAME

LAST NAME

ADDRESS

APT.#   CITY

STATE/PROV.   ZIP/POSTAL CODE

Visit us online at
www.ReaderService.com

seeing it. Other times it felt like a lifetime ago, almost as if he were a different man than the reckless kid who'd zipped along those country roads on a battered motor-cycle.

"Renae hasn't remarried?"

"No."

Caroline slanted him a sideways glance. "Is she still as pretty as you remembered?"

He gave her a look, but answered candidly. "Prettier."

She turned to face him fully. "So?"

Pushing his hands into the pockets of his leather jacket, he shrugged. "So—what?"

"What are you doing about it?"

"Caroline..."

"What?" she asked with a quizzical frown. "You just said it's been seven years, Evan. Do you really think you'd be betraying your friend to ask her out now, after all this time?"

He shrugged, uncertain how he felt about that, exactly. He hadn't allowed himself to dwell on what Jason might say at the prospect of his best friend and his wife being together. But he knew very well what Jason's mother would say.

"Renae lives with her mother-in-law. Lucy Sanchez," he said bluntly. "They're still very close."

"Oh." Caroline grimaced. "That could be a problem."

He sighed gustily. "You think?"

"They actually live together?"

"Yeah. Lucy moved in with Renae right after Jason died, and she's been there ever since."

"Wow. As fond as I am of my mother-in-law, I wouldn't want to live with her."

"Well, yeah, but Renae's always been crazy about

Lucy. I think she sees her as the replacement for the mother she lost when she was just a kid."

"That's sweet, of course, but even then..." Caroline shook her head. "I love our mother, but I wouldn't want to live with her as an adult."

Evan pushed at a pebble on the tidy walking path with his shoe. "They needed each other, I guess. And now it's just what they're used to."

"Oh, right. I guess Renae needed help with her babies. Twins, right?"

He nodded. "A boy and a girl. They're in first grade now."

"I'm sure they're very cute."

"I haven't met them," he admitted, "but I've seen pictures. They look a lot like Jason."

His sister eyed him closely. "Do you want to meet them?"

He'd asked himself that question a few times, too. So far when he'd been with Renae, except for that one meeting with Tate, he'd had her full attention. That would not be true when she was with the children she adored. Nor should it be.

He had never been involved with a single mother. Was he unselfish enough to accept that she would always put their needs ahead of his, ahead of her own—even though he totally agreed that was the way it should be?

"Yeah, I'd like to meet them."

He thought he could accept the kids. Heck, he liked kids. He didn't even think it would bother him that they bore such strong resemblance to their father. Jason had been his friend, and he was happy that Jason's legacy lived on.

The twins weren't the biggest obstacle between him and Renae.

Caroline had always had a spooky way of somehow following his thoughts. She cut straight to the heart of the biggest problem her brother faced. "What about Mrs. Sanchez? Have you spent any time with *her* since you and Renae have been getting together?"

"As far as I know, Renae hasn't even told Mrs. Sanchez she's been meeting with me."

"Ouch."

"Yeah," he said grimly. "That could get ugly."

Caroline rested a hand on his arm. "Do you still have feelings for Renae, Evan?"

He thought of the kiss he and Renae had shared when they had parted last week. The emotions that had flooded through him, the strength it took to let her leave…

"I see that you do," Caroline murmured before he could even answer.

"It's—" He hated to keep repeating himself, but he could think of only one thing to say. "It's complicated."

She patted his arm. "You know how to reach me if you ever want to talk."

He wasn't sure how to take that offer. Was she implying he would soon need consoling again because of Renae? That he was risking heartbreak by spending time with her? Or was he overreacting to a simple statement of support?

He wasn't accustomed to feeling so uncertain, so conflicted.

And he knew exactly who to thank for those feelings.

* * *

Renae was just about to turn in when her cell phone buzzed that evening. She didn't have to check the screen before answering. "Hello?"

"I hope it's not too late to call, but I wanted to wish you a last-minute happy Thanksgiving."

Though she told herself she hadn't been waiting for this call, she knew she wasn't being entirely honest. As much as she hated to admit it, she would have been disappointed if Evan hadn't called.

"It's not too late. How was your Thanksgiving with your family?"

"It was nice. I ate too much."

She laughed softly, aware of how quiet it was in her home where everyone slept but her. "So did I. But that's part of the holiday, I guess."

"Yeah. I didn't say I regretted it."

She chuckled again.

"Did the kids have a good time?" he asked, his voice a pleasant murmur in her ear.

She closed her eyes, picturing Evan in front of her as she answered. "They did. They were shamelessly indulged today. I'll probably have to remind them of a few rules tomorrow."

"You don't have to work tomorrow?"

"No, the office is closed to give us all a long week-end before the end-of-the-year-appointments madness."

"Tate and I let our crews take off today, but the rest of the weekend they'll be busy making sure all the Christmas displays we contracted are completed."

Supported by the pillows behind her back, Renae leaned against her headboard, drawing her knees up in front of her. She was already dressed in pajamas and the room was lit only by the dimmed lamp on the nightstand, adding an air of intimacy to the quiet conversation.

"Leslie insists we should put up our Christmas tree this weekend, because all her friends' families decorate their trees the weekend after Thanksgiving," she said dryly. "We use an artificial tree because of Lucy's allergies, so at least it won't be a fire hazard during the next month."

"If you need any help hanging lights or anything, you could always give me a call. For you—no charge," he said lightly.

Oh, yeah, like that was going to happen. He had to know she wouldn't call, but maybe he was only teasing with the offer.

"Thanks," she said, her tone matching his, "but we can manage the tree and a door wreath. We don't go overboard with holiday decorations, though the kids would probably love a big, splashy display."

"Yeah, well, you have my number if you change your mind."

She responded with a noncommittal mumble.

"Have you heard about that big walk-through holiday light display that's opening tomorrow night? The one at the community center?"

"Yes, of course." One of the small towns surrounding Little Rock had advertised the light display at their community center extensively. She planned to take the twins to see it.

"Price-Daugherty was responsible for designing and implementing it," he informed her. "Maybe you'd like to come to the lighting ceremony with me tomorrow?

Why don't you bring the kids? I think they'd get a kick out of it."

"I, uh—" She bit her lower lip. She'd convinced herself that Evan was teasing about offering to help her string lights, but this offer was unmistakable. Evan was actually suggesting that they have an outing with her kids.

She was so not ready for all the complications that would come with that. Fortunately, Renae had a genuine reason to decline Evan's invitation—this time.

"Thank you, but we've already made plans with Lucy tomorrow afternoon, and there's a kids' party tomorrow evening."

He sounded more resigned than displeased when he responded. "I understand. It was a last-minute invitation. Maybe we can do it some other time before Christmas?"

She bit her lip again, so hard she was half-surprised she didn't taste blood. She couldn't commit to any plans involving the twins until she talked to Lucy. And she wasn't ready to do that until she knew what was happening between her and Evan.

When her silence continued to stretch, Evan cleared his throat, the sound a low rumble through the phone. "I guess you're tired. We'll talk later. Have a nice day with your kids tomorrow."

"Thank you."

"I'll, uh, see you Wednesday?"

She told herself this was the perfect time to break it off with Evan—whatever "it" was. She'd gotten through the past week without seeing him, though not without thinking of him almost constantly. It would be better all around if they kept their future interactions focused solely on the scholarship.

Polite. Pleasant. Platonic.

It wasn't as if either of them had any real investment in this...well, she couldn't call it a relationship. Was it an affair? That didn't sound right, either.

"Renae?"

"It's going to be hectic at work next week, making up for these days off," she prevaricated.

She should have known he would have wanted a more specific response. Evan wasn't one to settle for vague hints. "Does that mean I *won't* see you Wednesday?"

Say the words, Renae. End it now.

She couldn't do it.

"I'll let you know," she said instead.

Though she sensed his dissatisfaction with her non-response, he said only, "All right. Good night, Renae."

"Good night."

She set the phone on the nightstand and turned off the lamp, leaving the room dark and silent. Turning onto her side, she could just see the outline of the empty pillow beside hers. She tried to remember how Jason had looked sprawled beside her in the darkness, but her memories had grown hazy with the passing years. She had never spent a night with Evan, never slept with him beside her—and yet it was all too easy to envision him lying there.

Guilt flooded through her, though she told herself it was an irrational reaction. Jason would not have expected her life to end with his. They had been so very young.

Would she feel this conflicted about anyone other

than Evan? Was her self-recrimination entirely rooted in the fact that she'd been unwillingly intrigued by Evan even before she'd married Jason?

She reminded herself, as she did so often, that she had never been unfaithful to Jason, that she had committed herself fully to making their marriage work, that she had loved her husband and had expected to spend the rest of her life with him. One impulsive kiss had not been a betrayal of him, nor had she spent the two years of her marriage fantasizing about Evan, though perhaps she had thought of him occasionally. The problems she and Jason had encountered had had nothing to do with anyone outside the two of them.

Despite those reassurances, she still believed she should keep an emotional barrier between herself and Evan. Partially because of those old conflicted emotions. Partially because of the inevitable complications between herself and Lucy. Partially because she hesitated to introduce anyone new into her children's lives without certainty about how that change would affect them.

But mostly because she was afraid for herself, she admitted finally, though she hated feeling like such a coward.

Every instinct inside her warned that Evan Daugherty could break her heart if she wasn't careful. And she'd had enough heartache in her past.

Maybe she'd been a little lonely at times in the past few years, but overall she'd made a comfortable, contented life for herself and her children. What kind of fool would she be to risk what she had achieved on a man who excited her, bewildered her, tempted her—and utterly terrified her with the seductive power he held over her?

Chapter Seven

Renae thought she had prepared for the crowds on the day after Thanksgiving—"black Friday," as it was known in retail parlance—especially since she wasn't trying to hit the big sales. Still, traffic was even more hectic than she had expected when she drove Lucy and the kids to a movie theater that afternoon, where they then stood in a long line with other holiday-hyper children. By the time the theater lights dimmed and the family-friendly film began to play, Renae gave a long sigh of relief that she wouldn't have to go back out for another hour and a half or so.

Fortunately, the crowds had thinned some by the time the movie ended. Renae figured the predawn shoppers had crashed for the remainder of the day with Thanksgiving leftovers and televised football games.

"We're still going ice-skating, aren't we, Mama?"

Leslie reminded as soon as she and her brother were strapped into the backseat of the car. "You promised."

"I remember." Exchanging wry glances with Lucy in the passenger seat, Renae started the car.

Several of the twins' friends would be gathering at the River Market Pavilion downtown that evening to admire the decorations and skate on the outdoor ice rink installed there through the holiday season. Glancing at the clock, Renae noted that they still had an hour before everyone was to meet. They'd be early, but there wasn't time to go home first, and she supposed they could stroll through the Market Hall until the others arrived, though the twins would surely beg for snacks from the many internationally themed food vendors who operated there.

Leslie and Daniel settled for cups of hot cocoa, topped with whipped cream and a little peppermint cane. The cocoa looked so good that Renae and Lucy each had a cup, as well, drinking them at a table inside the open Market Hall, which buzzed with shoppers, diners and visitors. Doors led out from the hall to the pavilions where the ice rink was now set up, but which hosted farmers' markets and merchandise vendors in the warmer months. Through the glass, they could see people already circling inside the rink.

Renae loved coming to the farmers' markets on Saturday mornings for fresh produce, and the kids always enjoyed coming with her to gape at the colorful displays of fruits, vegetables, herbs, breads and flowers. Many of the shoppers brought dogs on leashes—though Renae had refused to bring irrepressible Boomer into the crowds—and there were always street musicians and clowns and other entertainers to hold the twins' attention while Renae filled her market bags.

She had such a good life, she reminded herself, sipping her cocoa and watching the twins chattering happily with their grandmother as they waited impatiently for their friends to arrive. How could she possibly ask for more?

She glanced at her watch. "It's almost time to meet everybody at the ticket booth. Finished with your cocoa?"

The kids hopped up to toss their mostly empty cups into a trash bin.

"I'm going to duck into the ladies' room and then I'll come out to join you," Lucy said over her shoulder as she walked away.

Admonishing the twins not to dash away and get lost in the crowd, Renae threw out her cup and then turned toward the exit doors. Only to find herself directly in front of Evan Daugherty.

With a pretty brunette at his side.

Evan found Emma waiting for him at the west entrance to the Market Hall at just after 5:00 p.m. on Friday. She'd called earlier to ask if they could meet for a cup of coffee, saying she needed to talk to him about something. Though he'd been a bit surprised by the request, he had agreed immediately. She had suggested the River Market because she was joining friends afterward a block away. The River Market was also directly across the river from his apartment building, so he could be home in five minutes after their meeting.

"Besides," she had added, "the River Market is cheerful, and I need that today."

Mildly alarmed, he'd hurried to meet her at the time she'd set. He had known Emma almost a year and he'd never heard her sound so troubled. Of course, he and Emma hadn't spent any time alone together, meeting only once a week at lunch with Tate, Kim and Lynette, so he couldn't say he knew her all that well, really. Still, he considered her a friend, and he tried to be available whenever his friends needed him.

She greeted him with a smile that looked a bit strained. "Thank you for meeting me, Evan."

Aware that several male observers were watching him with envy, Evan took Emma's outstretched hand. "Of course."

Emma was an attractive woman. Her near-black hair fell straight to her shoulders, framing an oval face with flawless, creamy skin. Her dark eyes were slightly almond-shaped, and she had a figure that made men stop dead in their tracks. Being a healthy male with normal vision, Evan had taken note of all these things the first time he'd met her. And yet, he'd never even considered asking her out.

Maybe it was the way they'd become acquainted, through the casual group of friends who shared lunch every Wednesday. Not exactly conducive to flirtation— though that hadn't stopped Tate and Kim from falling in love. Maybe it was the fact that he'd known from the start that Emma wasn't the breezy-no-strings-fling type, and that was all he'd had to offer any woman for the past near decade.

Whatever his own reasons, he was pretty sure that Emma didn't have feelings for him, either. She must have a good reason for wanting to meet him alone this way, but whatever it was, it had nothing to do with romance.

"Let's go inside and grab a table," he said, reaching for the door. "Maybe we'll luck out and find a corner where we can talk."

A gaggle of young teens headed for the ice rink dashed through the door when he opened it, but he and Emma managed to avoid being mowed down. They entered side by side, heading for the coffee shop at the other end of the holiday-decorated hall lined with food and gifts vendors. Tables were arranged down the center of the hall, but Evan thought it would be quieter at the back, making conversation easier.

They were just over halfway to their destination when he came face-to-face with Renae.

While he adjusted to his shock at seeing her there, he saw her gaze dart from him to Emma and then back again. It wasn't hard to guess what she was thinking.

"Renae," he said, giving her an easy smile, trying to look as though he hadn't just been knocked for a loop by the very sight of her. "This is a surprise."

Her own smile was notably forced. "Hello, Evan."

He glanced at the children bouncing impatiently on either side of her. Seeing young Daniel in person was even more of a jolt than seeing his photograph had been. The boy looked exactly like Jason. Leslie bore a strong resemblance, as well, but her features were softer, more feminine.

At least Lucy was nowhere in sight.

Remembering his manners, he glanced at his curious companion. "Emma Grainger, this is Renae Sanchez and her kids, Daniel and Leslie."

Before the women could do more than nod in response to the introduction, Daniel asked, "I don't know you. How do you know our names?"

Renae put a hand on her son's shoulder. "Daniel, mind your manners. This is Mr. Daugherty. He's a friend."

Leslie was studying Evan's face with an intensity that looked older than her years, and made her look much more like her mother, despite their different coloring. "I saw your picture. You were my daddy's friend."

He felt his eyebrows rise a little, but he nodded. "Yes, I was."

"Are you here to go skating? We're going to skate with some of our friends."

Evan didn't have a lot of experience talking to kids, but he figured it was just like talking to anyone else. "No, we're not here to skate. My friend and I met here for a cup of coffee."

Leslie nodded, but couldn't seem to resist saying, "Skating's more fun. And you should try the hot chocolate. It's good, isn't it, Mama?"

"Yes, it is."

"It's very nice to meet you, Renae," Emma said then. "Has Evan told you that my family would like to make a contribution to the scholarship?"

"He did, and we appreciate it very much," Renae replied graciously, though her tone was still a bit more formal than usual.

Emma smiled at the children, speaking to them both. "I'm sure you'll enjoy skating. We never had outdoor ice-skating in Arkansas when I was your age, and I always thought it looked like fun."

Leslie nodded eagerly. "We go to the indoor rink sometimes, but we wanted to come here today. We like to skate. Even if Grammy says we have to wear our bike helmets."

Evan had just processed the meaning of that slightly aggrieved statement when Lucy Sanchez appeared. "Renae, I thought you were taking the children out to—"

Lucy's words died when she saw who stood in front of her daughter-in-law. Her round face paled.

He injected as much warmth as he could into his voice. "Hello, Mrs. Sanchez."

Lucy put a hand on her granddaughter's shoulder and drew the child back against her as if protecting her from a possible mugger. "Evan," she acknowledged frostily.

"Lucy, this is Emma Grainger," Renae said quickly. "She's the one I told you about whose family is having a fundraising auction for Jason's scholarship."

Nodding to Emma with a little more graciousness than she had displayed toward Evan, Lucy murmured, "That's very kind of you and your family. My son would be grateful."

"Mama, I think I see Jacob out there." Tugging at his mother's hand, Daniel pointed toward the exit door through which they could see the skating rink. "They don't know we're here."

"We really should go on out," Lucy urged. "I'm sure they're waiting for us."

While that was probably true, Evan knew Lucy was mostly just trying to get her family away from him. Because that irked him, he gave her a bright smile. "It was nice seeing you again, Mrs. Sanchez."

She muttered something unintelligible in response and led her granddaughter toward the exit. Leslie looked back over her shoulder to wave a goodbye to Evan and Emma.

With Daniel still pulling at her hand, Renae gave Evan an apologetic look, but said only, "It was nice to meet you, Emma."

"I'll call you," Evan said quietly to her, making sure his words didn't carry to the hastily departing Lucy.

She nodded and kept walking.

He couldn't dwell on that awkward encounter now—he had to focus on the friend who needed his attention. "Let's get that coffee," he said to Emma, waving a hand toward the counter.

A few minutes later, they sat in chrome-and-plastic chairs at a small, laminate-topped round table in the quietest corner they could find. Sipping his coffee black, Evan watched as Emma stirred creamer into her mug, her expression distracted.

It was hard not to be distracted himself. Was Renae skating with the twins? He'd like to see her on skates, laughing with her kids. Was she thinking of him now, aware of his proximity? Trying not to frown, he hoped that awareness wasn't dimming Renae's fun. He certainly hadn't meant to ruin her outing.

Emma glanced up at him. "Lucy Sanchez is no fan of yours."

Had she somehow followed his line of thinking? His chuckle held little humor. "Picked up on that, did you?"

"I didn't expect that," she admitted. "I thought everyone liked you."

"That's very nice of you, but I have my share of detractors. Lucy just happens to head the list."

"I'm surprised. I'd have thought she would be grateful to you for establishing the scholarship."

He shrugged. "More likely she's gratified by the scholarship despite my involvement."

"I don't understand it. You're such a nice guy."

Emma wasn't the type who would pry for details, and he wasn't in the mood to discuss Lucy just then. Instead, he turned the conversation to Emma. "You said you needed to talk to me, Emma. Is it about the scholarship?"

She shook her head. "Actually, I called you because you were in the army. And because you've always had such good advice when the rest of us discussed problems during lunches."

That was certainly not what he'd expected to hear. "You're not thinking of enlisting, are you?"

She smiled fleetingly. "Not exactly. Was it hard for you? Leaving your home and your family here, I mean, to go off to another part of the world on your own?"

Taking her question in the same serious vein in which it was asked, he nodded. "Yeah. It was. My first time away from home, really, and I have to admit I was nervous. Had plenty of times when I got homesick. But it was something I needed to do."

He hadn't enlisted only to run away from his feelings for his friend's fiancée, he assured himself. There had been a number of reasons he'd felt obligated to serve, and that had been only one of them.

"I've never lived anywhere but here," Emma admitted. "Never more than thirty miles from my parents. I've had an offer for a job that would give me a chance to live in an entirely different part of the country and work with a former military man. I've been warned that he'll be a challenge but I'm still tempted. I thought I'd run the offer past you and see what you think on both counts."

She made a little face when she added, "I haven't talked with my parents about it yet. I already know they're not going to like it. I tried to talk to Lynette, but she doesn't want me to leave the rehab center, even though I told her I'd probably come back eventually. I'm sure I could get my job there back. I just, well, I just feel like I need to try something different, you know?"

He thought he understood now why she'd called him. She needed someone who knew her, but could remain objective, maybe just listen to her deliberations without having an overly emotional response.

He leaned back more comfortably in his chair, doing his best to put Renae out of his mind for now. He would call her when he got home. He wanted to make sure she knew that while he had made himself available for Emma today, Renae was the only woman he considered more than just a friend.

Chapter Eight

The kids were in bed that evening, Lucy was in her room, and Renae sat in her own bedroom, propped against her headboard and staring at the book in her lap. She'd been holding the book for maybe ten minutes without even opening it, figuring she would be unable to concentrate on the story, no matter how good it might be.

Her phone sat on the nightstand within easy reach. She found her gaze drifting that way repeatedly, and it annoyed her that she sat here waiting for a phone call. She could pretend all she wanted that she'd come into her room for quiet reading time, but lying to herself would serve no purpose. Every muscle in her body was braced for a call from Evan.

Still she jumped when the phone vibrated against the nightstand. Feeling even more like a fool, she snatched it up. "Hello?"

"How was the ice?"

Why on earth would the sound of Evan's voice bring a lump to her throat and make her eyes burn with a hint of tears? She forced herself to answer lightly, hoping there was no hint of emotional turmoil in her succinct response. "Cold."

He chuckled, but she wondered if his humor was just a bit strained. "Yeah, I figured. Did the kids have fun?"

"They had a great time."

It had been a magical setting in the twins' eyes, with the colored lights strung in the pavilion above them, the Arkansas River running alongside, inky beneath the starlit sky, reflecting the lights of the cities lining its banks. Had she not been so conscious of Evan sitting inside with the beautiful Emma Grainger, Renae would have been as enchanted as her kids by the cheery holiday atmosphere. As it was, she had worked hard to concentrate solely on her children, snapping photos, laughing with them, cheering them on as they'd played on the ice. Lucy, too, had made an effort to keep up a happy front for the kids, though Renae could tell that seeing Evan had dimmed her mood considerably.

"I had no idea you'd be at the River Market this evening."

"I know. I didn't mention it to you."

"Just didn't want you to think I deliberately arranged that encounter. Emma needed to ask my advice about a quandary she's having, and that was just a convenient spot for us to meet."

"I never thought you expected to see me," she assured him, remembering the surprise on Evan's face when he'd seen her. She thought there had also been pleasure in his eyes at the sight of her, but then Lucy had made her appearance.

"I hope running into me didn't spoil your outing."

"Of course not. Why would it have?" she asked, deliberately obtuse.

He didn't let her get away with it. "I could see that Lucy hates me now as much as she did seven years ago."

Lucy had not mentioned Evan since. Not in the car on the way home, not while the twins were preparing for bed, nor when Lucy had announced that she was turning in early. When Renae had tried to bring up the incident, Lucy had cut her off with a shake of her head, making it clear she wasn't ready to discuss it. As much as Renae loved her mother-in-law, she was aware that Lucy could be very stubborn.

"Lucy doesn't hate you, Evan." At least, Renae didn't think Lucy's antipathy could be described as hatred. It was just that Lucy still identified Evan with grief and loss. As unfair as that might be to Evan, Renae wasn't really sure how to change Lucy's mindset.

"Hmm." It was obvious he didn't believe her, and she supposed she couldn't blame him for that.

Because there was nothing more to say about Lucy, she changed the subject. "Emma seemed nice."

"She is. I consider her a good friend."

The way he emphasized the last word made her think he was assuring her that there was nothing more than friendship between himself and Emma. Not that it was any of Renae's concern, of course.

"Anyway," he said when the silence stretched a bit too long, "I just wanted to tell you it was good to see you today, and I'm sorry I made things awkward for you with Lucy."

"It's okay."

"So, what about lunch Wednesday? Want to join Tate and me with our friends so you can get to know them before the party?"

She moistened her lips. "This is a very busy time at the clinic. I'm not sure I can get away for lunch on Wednesday."

"That's cool," he assured her, his tone studiedly casual. "But you're welcome, if you're able. And if not, I'll be at my place at the usual time Wednesday evening."

Renae leaned her head back against the headboard and stared at the ceiling, wishing she could find words of wisdom written there. "This is getting too complicated, Evan. I don't really know what to do."

"Seems pretty simple to me. Do you want to see me again?"

"It's not that easy."

"I know there are issues, but the question still stands."

Issues. She guessed that was one way of putting it.

"Renae? Do you?"

"Yes," she said with a sigh.

She heard the satisfaction in his voice when he said, "You know where to find me."

"You aren't making this any less confusing for me."

"I want to be with you. I think I've made that clear enough. The next move is up to you."

"And if I decide it's just too problematic? We can just go back to being comfortable friends, like you and Emma?"

"You and I have never been comfortable friends,

Renae. We tried, and it didn't work. I don't see it happening now."

Her fingers tightened around the phone in response to his somber comment. "And you think this will work? This...what would you call it, Evan?"

"Maybe it's about time we talk about that."

A ripple of panic coursed through her. "I—"

"Not now. But the next time we're together."

She exhaled quietly. She really wasn't ready for that talk just now, though it was becoming inevitable if she and Evan were going to continue to see each other. Unless she carefully avoided talking to him by making sure she and Evan weren't alone together again, of course.

Coward.

"Good night, Renae. Call if you need me for anything."

She knew he meant that. Just as she knew it was very unlikely that she would call. "Good night, Evan."

Returning her phone to the nightstand, she groaned and buried her face in her hands, feeling more torn than ever between the two facets of her personality that had emerged in the past weeks. She knew she should focus on her responsible, dutiful, maternal side—but she wasn't sure how easy it would be to put that long-neglected adventurous, impetuous and sensual part of herself back into the mental closet where it had been safely hidden for so long.

"Ouch."

Evan froze midcaress, in response to Renae's involuntary grimace. "What? Did I hurt you? What's wrong?"

Sheepishly, she eased her left arm from around his neck. "Sorry. It's a little bruised."

"Let me see."

"Oh, well, I—"

But he had already eased her purple cardigan from her shoulders, leaving her arms bared by the sleeveless purple-and-gray-striped sweater she'd worn beneath. The color of her outfit coincidentally matched the deep eggplant blotch that spread from her elbow almost halfway to her shoulder on the outside of her left arm.

"What in hell did you do to yourself?"

She made a face, instinctively attempting to cover the bruise with her other hand. "It's a long story."

She'd arrived at his apartment only a few minutes earlier after several days of debating with herself, and several hours of being convinced that this time she would finally be strong enough to stay away. She'd gotten into her car thinking she would maybe go visit her favorite bookstore, but when she'd reached Evan's apartment complex, she'd turned into the parking lot in resignation, knowing she'd simply been fooling herself all along.

For all Evan's warnings about how they needed to talk, he had barely let her into his living room before he had her in his arms.

But now he was more focused on her injury. He moved her hand out of the way and traced a fingertip lightly over the bruise, barely making contact with her skin. Still, it was enough to make her shiver.

"Looks bad. Does it hurt?"

She craned her neck to look at the arm. "Not too much. And it actually looks better than it did. It's fading some."

"When did you do it? How?"

She laughed softly, ruefully. "It was one of those silly TV sitcom moments. A stepladder, a pair of overexcited twins and a hyperactive dog."

"You fell?"

"I caught myself before I hit the floor. But I smacked my arm on a cabinet when I flung it out to steady myself."

"What were you doing on a ladder?"

"Putting a star on the top of the tree. It would have been fine if Daniel had left the dog outside, as I'd instructed him to do. He spent some time in his room reflecting on why he should do what he's told."

Evan bent his head to press his lips to her shoulder. "Did you see a doctor?" he asked, his mouth moving against her skin.

"Um…" She swallowed, her eyelids going heavy. "No, it was just a bruise."

"I told you I'd help you with the decorations."

Her eyes flew open. She drew a few inches away from him. "You know why that isn't going to happen."

Evan sighed, impatience radiating from him.

"Besides," she added quickly, "I'm perfectly capable of decorating my own tree. Next time, the dog will stay outside."

There was still a frown in his eyes, but his hand was very gentle when he stroked it down her arm. "You've got a couple hours free, right?"

She nodded. "Lucy and the kids won't be home until eight. She puts them to bed if I stay out after their bedtime, which isn't often, but occasionally."

He picked up her cardigan and held it for her. "Let's get out of here."

She was too surprised to resist as he helped her into the sweater. "Where are we going?"

"Out."

"But—"

"Look, if we stay here, we both know how we're going to end up spending the time," he said flatly. "If we go for a drive or a burger or something, at least we can talk some."

She wasn't sure what unnerved her more—the thought of staying in with him or going out with him. But she let him help her into her coat and followed him out.

Though Evan drove a dual-cab pickup truck for practical business reasons, it was a nice vehicle with cushy seats and a beautifully appointed dashboard. It suited him. "Jingle Bells" played from his radio when he started the engine. His smile a little embarrassed, he turned down the volume. "Guess I got carried away with the season. Normally, you'd be hearing something suitably edgy and masculine in my truck, I assure you."

She laughed and fastened her seat belt.

This was beginning to feel very much like a date, she realized abruptly, her laughter fading. Some people might say it was about time, considering everything— but now she was suddenly nervous. Silly, maybe, but true—and it was that exciting kind of nervous that made her fingers tingle, her skin warm, her toes curl in her shoes. He slanted a smile at her and her breath caught. Yes, this was nice—and terrifying.

"Um…" She pushed her voice through her tight throat. "Where, exactly, are we going?"

"We have a few choices. We could go to a restaurant. We could see a movie. We could go bowling. We could drop in on a party one of my friends is hosting tonight. I have an open invitation."

"Bowling?" she asked with a smile.

"Is that your choice?"

"No, it's a question. Are you a bowler?"

"I think the last time I bowled was in college. It just popped into my head. But I'm game if you are."

Renae laughed. "Let's eat—I'm hungry."

They decided on a quiet Japanese restaurant Evan recommended. The lights were almost a little too dim, but the atmosphere was peaceful and the food was excellent. Because of their public setting, they kept the conversation light and casual, and their easy discussion of books, movies and current events only reinforced the date-night feeling.

Those more troubling issues between them were still there, of course, simmering just below the surface of their comfortable prattle. But for that leisurely hour, Renae allowed herself to enjoy the novelty of sitting across a candlelit table from a handsome man, enjoying grown-up conversation. They shared a sinfully rich chocolate mousse cake for dessert, leaning toward the center of the little table so that their heads were close together, laughing softly as they scooped up bites with their spoons.

After dinner, he drove her around town to admire some of the light displays Price-Daugherty had been commissioned to design while holiday music played softly in the cab of the truck. He seemed in no hurry to return to his apartment. All too aware of passing time, Renae tried not to think too far ahead but instead appreciate each moment of this very pleasant outing.

They had to head back eventually, of course. A silence fell between them as he drove across the I-30 bridge spanning the Arkansas River. His apartment building lay just ahead and she studied it somberly, trying to pick out his windows. He parked, then turned to study her in the pale security lighting.

"Do you have a little more time?"

The dashboard clock informed her that it was just before eight. They'd eaten early and hadn't been out all that long. She could send a quick text to Lucy that she'd be a little later tonight. But still...

"Maybe I'd better go," she said softly, giving him an unguarded look. "I'm afraid if I come up, I'll be tempted to stay too long."

He reached out to toy with her hair, tucking a strand behind her ear. "You wouldn't see me rushing you out."

"That doesn't help," she chided, though she couldn't resist rubbing her cheek against his hand.

He turned his hand so he was cradling her face in his palm. "I'm not ready for you to go home."

"I've had a very nice time," she admitted.

"I've enjoyed it, too." Evan leaned closer to brush a kiss across her mouth.

She clutched the collar of his shirt, her lips responding to his. His kisses were familiar now, but each still thrilled. She knew his taste, his feel, his scent, and still she wanted more.

Several long, heated kisses later, he lifted his head with a groan, shifting his weight to ease a cramped leg. "I'm too old for making out in the parking lot."

Renae was surprised to hear a giggle escape her. "Apparently not."

A smile flashed across his face in the shadowy truck

cab. "Oh, well, if any of my neighbors saw, I probably just gained a few extra stud points."

"Unless they heard 'Jingle Bells' playing from your radio earlier."

He made a face at her. "Funny."

"I'd better go," she said with a wistful sigh. "Thank you for the lovely evening, Evan."

He kissed her again, slowly, but drew away without trying to change her mind. "I'll call you."

She nodded and reached for her door.

His hand fell on her shoulder. "Renae."

"Yes?"

"That party Emma's family is giving Saturday evening? I'd like you to go with me."

"I said I would be there," she reminded him. "I promised to represent the scholarship fund with you and Tate and Kim."

He shook his head. "I don't mean I want you to attend as part of the group. I want you to go with me."

"Oh." She bit her lip, suddenly realizing what he was asking. "You mean, like a date?"

He shrugged. "If that's what you want to call it."

So he had viewed tonight much the same way she had—as a shift in their...well, *relationship* was the only word she could come up with.

"I could meet you there," she said, though she wasn't sure he would be satisfied with that offer.

She was right.

"I'd rather pick you up, so we can go in together."

She twisted her fingers in her lap. "You know what you're asking of me."

Holding her eyes steadily, he nodded. "You have to tell her sometime, Renae."

"Do I?" she murmured.

After a pause, he asked, "Did you think we could just keep doing this indefinitely? Meeting on Wednesdays for a couple hours of lovemaking or maybe an occasional secret dinner out without Lucy ever being the wiser?"

She sighed ruefully. "It had crossed my mind."

"As much as I've enjoyed having you to myself these past few weeks, it's time to decide where we're going from here. I'm thinking a first step would be for us to see each other openly. We got a start on that tonight, but maybe the party would be a chance for us to take it a step further."

Renae had been relatively confident tonight that they wouldn't run into anyone who knew them. What Evan was suggesting was a far bigger step than having dinner in a dimly lit, out-of-the-way restaurant.

And she didn't know if she was ready.

"I'd have to think about it. I'd have to decide what to tell Lucy."

His dark brows furrowed. "How about telling her you choose your own friends?"

Friends? She could figure out what to say if she and Evan were simply friends. Surely he understood how much more difficult it would be to tell Jason's mother that she was sleeping with the enemy.

Not that she would be quite that blunt about it, of course. But Lucy could be a little too perceptive.

"Just let me think about it, okay?"

"You do that."

He sounded grumpy, and that wasn't the way she wanted to end the evening. But she wasn't going to make rash promises just to appease him, either. He might as well accept that now.

She reached again for the door. "I really do have to go now."

He met her at the back of the truck and walked her to her car. He waited until she'd unlocked her door, then slipped a hand behind her head and gave her a long, thorough kiss that left her clinging to the car for balance when her knees threatened to buckle.

"Think about that, too," he advised her, stepping away.

Swallowing hard, she slid into her driver's seat. Evan closed the door for her, then walked away without waiting for her to start the engine.

Looking after him, she felt a mixture of frustration and fear. Evan Daugherty had always aroused strong emotions in her, and that wasn't changing as they spent more time together. In fact, it was growing worse.

She was going to have to make some hard decisions where Evan was concerned—soon. She wanted to believe that there was no question what choice she would make if it came down to Lucy or Evan.

But the thought of watching Evan walk out of her life was almost more than she could bear.

Which left her...where?

Trying to catch up on some paperwork that had accumulated during an especially hectic day, Renae stayed a little late at work on Thursday. She called to let Lucy know she'd be delayed and not to hold dinner for her. She would make it up to the kids this weekend, she vowed. She'd promised to take them to see Santa at the mall Saturday morning, and while she wasn't looking forward to the crowds, she knew the kids would enjoy the holiday bustle.

Cathy, too, stayed after hours, claiming she had some extra work of her own to complete. Renae suspected her coworker simply didn't want to leave Renae working late alone, though Cathy refused to admit that was her motivation.

They sat side by side at computers, Renae answering correspondence and dealing with insurance claims while Cathy entered billing information and cleaned up the appointments calendar for the next week. For a few minutes after their last coworker walked out, the only sound in the clinic was the clatter of dueling keyboards.

Cathy was the first to speak. "So, how have your scholarship meetings been going, Renae? Getting a lot done on it?"

"Yes, we're ready to accept applications. We'll name the recipients in April."

"It feels really good to be involved with such a worthy cause, doesn't it?"

Cathy was active in several local charitable organizations herself, so she spoke from experience. Renae nodded. "Yes, it does."

"Not to mention working on the cause with such a good-looking man. You are still working with Mr. Hottie, aren't you?"

Renae slanted her a look. "Don't start."

Her expression sobering, Cathy turned in her swivel chair to study Renae more closely. "You know I consider you a friend as well as a coworker, right? I mean, you were there for me when Joe and I broke up in July, and I really appreciated that."

Renae looked away from her monitor. "Of course

we're friends. Is there something you need to talk about?"

"Not me. You. I just want you to know you can talk to me if you need to."

Her fingers tripped on the keyboard, bringing up a string of nonsense on the screen.

"I'm fine, Cathy, but thank you for the offer."

Pushing a strand of frizzy red hair out of her face, Cathy gave her a chiding look. "Like I said, we're friends. I can tell when you're troubled. I mean, you've been sort of teetering between giddy and perturbed the past few weeks, which, in my vast thirty-nine years of experience, is usually a sign of a problematic new relationship."

"I haven't been giddy," Renae refuted immediately, uncomfortable with the word.

"Okay, maybe not giddy," Cathy conceded, "but definitely distracted, and in a good way."

Renae sighed. "It's—"

"—complicated," Cathy finished with her. "Honey, it always is."

"My mother-in-law blames Mr. Hottie, as you call him, for causing her son's death," Renae blurted. "She doesn't even know I've been meeting with him, much less—well, that there would be any possibility of anything more."

"Oh." Cathy blinked. "Um, wow."

"Yeah." Grimly, Renae cleared her screen and entered the correct data.

"Why would she blame—Evan, isn't it?"

Renae nodded without pausing in her work. "It was Evan who helped Jason buy a motorcycle a few years before the accident, to Lucy's disapproval. And Evan was the one who talked Jason into going for that last ride, even though Jason had originally made other plans. Evan made it safely through the intersection only moments before Jason followed and was hit by the car. So Lucy decided that Jason would still be alive if it weren't for Evan."

"Wow," Cathy said again, apparently at a loss for another word.

Renae nodded again and hit a few keys with a bit more force than necessary.

"I take it you don't agree with her?"

"Of course not. Evan would never have done anything deliberately to hurt Jason," Renae insisted.

Cathy eyed her with a frown. "Hmm."

Renae wasn't sure what she meant by that murmur, but she didn't ask for clarification.

After another few minutes of working in silence, Cathy said, "I know you're very close to your mother-in-law, but are you really willing to stop seeing a man you're interested in just to keep her happy?"

"I think the question should be, am I really willing to risk alienating a woman who has been like a mother to me for a decade over what could prove to be a passing attraction to a man who only showed up in my life again a couple of months ago?"

"Well, when you put it that way…"

"When I put it that way, the answer is obvious," Renae said with a renewed determination, struck by her own reasoning.

"But maybe—"

"I appreciate your concern, Cathy, really, but I need to finish up here so I can get home. Lucy and the kids are waiting for me."

"Okay, but if you want to talk, the offer stands."

"Thanks. I appreciate it." And she did, really—but this was a problem Renae knew she was going to have to resolve for herself.

Evan hadn't been exactly enthusiastic about the compromise Renae had suggested for the party, but he'd made the best of it, greeting her with a kiss when she arrived at his apartment. They would still walk into the event together, but she simply hadn't been comfortable with him picking her up at her house.

"You look great," he told her, stepping back to admire the total effect of her outfit. She'd obsessed a little over what to wear, finally settling on flowing black evening pants and a sparkly black-and-silver top with a deep scoop neckline and three-quarter sleeves. Conservative, but figure-flattering; classic, but with just a touch of bling for the holidays. The appreciation in Evan's eyes made her feel that her choice had been worth the dithering.

"You look very tasty, yourself," she assured him, eying his dark suit and holiday-red tie in approval. Evan could definitely rock a suit.

Drawing her gaze from him, she uttered a sound of surprise when she saw the Christmas tree displayed in front of his big window that overlooked the river. "Oh, how pretty."

Before she even touched the blue spruce's dense needles, she could tell by the scent that it was real. Tiny white LED lights glittered among the thick branches and reflected off delicate glass ornaments in red, gold and silver. A gold star sat proudly at the top of the tree, almost touching the ceiling. She couldn't help thinking how much more elegant this perfectly coordinated tree looked compared to the big artificial tree at home, covered haphazardly with multicolored lights, a hodge-podge of ornaments collected through the years and a few crafts-project ornaments made by the twins. While Evan's tree was perfection, she decided she preferred her own.

She wondered how he would view her kid-friendly decorations. And whether seeing them would make him, like her, wonder how their very different lives would mesh. "Your tree is beautiful," she said, pushing those disconcerting thoughts away. "Did you decorate it your-self or hire someone to do it?"

He shrugged, looking a little self-conscious. "I was at loose ends one evening, so I decided to put up a tree. I don't always bother, but I thought you might like it."

She moistened her lips. "You did this for me?"

"Well, I enjoy it, too, but—yeah. Mostly for you. I don't have many other visitors."

She was both incredibly touched and a bit discon-certed by his gesture. Every time she left him here, she wasn't sure she would be back, but Evan had gone to a lot of trouble on the assumption that she would be here to appreciate his efforts. Was he that confident that she wouldn't be able to stay away?

Or had he simply hoped she would not?

Evan glanced at his watch. "Are you ready to go?"

"Yes." She was a little nervous about this party but she figured she might as well make the best of it.

He heaved an exaggerated sigh. "I'd rather stay here with you, but I guess I'm ready, too."

"Knowing how you hate parties, I'm not sure that's

such a compliment to me," she teased, walking away from the tree.

He caught her around the waist and pulled her to him for a kiss that almost rattled her teeth. "Trust me," he said huskily when he released her, "it was a compliment."

Blinking somewhat dazedly, she followed him out the door.

Evan helped her into his truck, then rounded the front to the driver's door. While he settled into his seat, Renae lowered the passenger-side sunshade mirror to repair her lipstick.

"Did you tell Lucy where you're going tonight?" Evan asked as he stopped at the exit of the parking lot.

"Of course. I told her I was going to the party where her afghan's being auctioned."

"Did you tell her you were going with me?"

Renae cleared her throat. "I told her we were both attending."

"But not together."

Lucy had been disapproving enough that Renae would be at the same function as Evan. "He just keeps turning up," she had muttered. "Like a bad penny."

"I just want to help raise donations for the scholarship," Renae had replied, unable to quite meet her mother-in-law's eyes. "Tate and his wife and sister will be there, too. And a lot of other people."

All of which had been true, of course. So why did she feel vaguely guilty?

"I don't really want to talk about Lucy now," she said, toying with her evening bag.

"Fine. Neither do I."

"Fine." Renae gazed out the side window at the passing holiday lights, trying to put her self-recriminations out of her mind and get into the mood for a party.

The event was held in the ballroom of a local country club. It was immediately apparent that the Graingers were a prominent local family. Though Renae didn't usually travel in these circles, she recognized a few of the faces entering the extravagantly decorated room from local political and society news coverage.

"Wow," Evan murmured in Renae's ear. "When Emma said her family was throwing a 'little holiday party,' this wasn't exactly what I pictured."

A little less confident in her choice of clothing now, she glanced around warily, but finally decided she'd chosen well enough. The fashion choices ranged from dressy denim with sequins to holiday gowns, which put her somewhere in between. Maybe her outfit had come from a clearance rack after last year's holiday season, but at least it was from a quality line, she assured herself, needing the little private pep talk.

Emma must have been watching for them. With Tate and two other women trailing behind her, she threaded her way through the milling crowd to approach them with a warm smile. She looked stunning in a deep red side-gathered dress with a low neckline. Renae couldn't help wondering how Evan could have spent so much time around Emma without wanting to be more than just friends, but she supposed there was no explaining sexual chemistry.

Emma raised her voice a little to be heard clearly over the clamor of voices and laughter and the secular holiday music in the background. "Renae, it's so good to see you again."

Few people watching would probably guess that

Emma had met Renae only fleetingly on one previous occasion, Renae thought, returning the smile. "It's nice to see you, too, Emma."

Evan brushed a rather brotherly kiss against Emma's cheek. "You clean up pretty good, kid," he teased her.

She patted his arm. "As do you. Renae, you know Tate, of course. This is his wife, Kim, and his sister, Lynette. And this is Lynette's friend Ken Kelly," she added, motioning toward a tall, slender man standing a bit back from the rest of the group. "Everyone, say hello to Renae Sanchez."

The other two women nodded greetings. Kim had wavy, shoulder-length chestnut hair and brown eyes, just a hint of freckles across a cute nose, and a smile that was disarmingly gamine. Lynette had the same hazel-green eyes as her brother, set in a friendly, girl-next-door face. Her hair was loosely curled, the dark red color probably salon-enhanced.

"It's nice to finally meet you, Renae," Lynette said, studying her with open curiosity. "I've heard about you for years, of course, but our paths just never crossed."

"Come see our auction tables," Emma urged, motioning toward them all. "My mom and I set them up earlier and we're quite proud of them."

The red-and-green-draped tables lined a back wall of the room. The items available in the silent auction were beautifully displayed with pads and pens arranged so that guests could leave their bids. A list of the four charities that would benefit from the auction was displayed on a cheery poster on the wall. The Jason Sanchez Memorial Scholarship was second on the list. Her gaze lingering on the name for a moment, Renae felt a small lump in her throat as she thought of how touched Jason would be.

The variety of auction items was impressive, from the designer sunglasses donated by Renae's bosses to weekends at Arkansas fishing resorts, gift certificates for meals, services and merchandise, autographed sports memorabilia, and other attractive prizes. The Graingers were obviously well connected to have procured all these nice donations. It gratified Renae to see Lucy's snowy-white lap blanket displayed with special care, temptingly draped as though to illustrate how comfy it would be. Already several bids were written on the pad.

"I'm hoping to win that myself," Emma confided in a low voice to Renae. "I'm going to wait until the last minute, then 'snipe' my own bid onto the sheet. It will be fair—Dad will let everyone know when the bidding's about to come to an end. But I'm determined to get that lovely lap blanket."

Renae laughed. "We have quite a few of them at home. If this one gets away from you, I'll see what I can do to get you one."

"No, it's the principle of the thing now. I want this one."

"She's very competitive," Lynette said with a grin that slowly faded. "I'm going to miss her so much."

"Now, Lynette, don't start," Emma warned quickly, looking around to see if anyone else at the party had overheard. "Especially where my mom might hear you. She's having a hard enough time dealing with this—I don't want her to make a scene at the party."

Seeing that Renae looked confused, Evan explained in a low voice. "Emma's taking a leave of absence from her job at the rehab center to take a temporary job on the West Coast after the first of the year. Her friends and family are having trouble accepting her decision."

Emma sighed and shook her head. "I'm not moving away forever. I just want to experience something different for once in my life. On my own."

Lynette didn't look notably cheered. "Everything's changing," she grumbled. "It's hard for me to process change."

Tate laughed and patted his sister's back. "Deal with it, sis. Nothing stays the same forever, no matter how much you wish it would."

Unexpectedly struck by his words, Renae swallowed hard. She'd been struggling with her own fear of change since Evan had come back into her life. She understood all too well that changes could be both thrilling and unnerving—exactly the way she felt right now. It was a relief when Emma nudged them all into the crowd to start mingling.

Chapter Nine

The evening was more pleasant than Renae had expected. Though she met quite a few people during the course of the party, her time was spent primarily with Evan's group of close friends. She liked Emma, Kim and Lynette very much, talking with them very easily considering they had just met. She and Kim talked about their children, sharing funny stories of that first year of child rearing while Tate and Evan did some networking with a couple of local business bigwigs. Lynette's companion, Ken, stood by one of the food tables, chatting with another acquaintance, giving the four women a chance to visit over glasses of champagne.

"I can't imagine having two infants to take care of," Kim said with an impressed shake of her head. "It's been challenging enough with just one, especially with a full-time job, too. I went back to work when Daryn was six weeks old, putting her in an excellent day care program a friend had recommended. Tate and I married in October, and he's been great to help with her, but I was on my own for her first ten months. I don't know how I'd have gotten by with twins."

Renae had heard a little of the story of Tate's whirlwind courtship with the pretty single mom, but she was still curious about some of the details. She didn't ask, of course, merely responding to Kim's comments.

"I was lucky enough to have my mother-in-law to help me with the babies, or I don't know how I'd have coped. I was six months pregnant with them when I lost my husband, so I didn't have long to prepare for them afterward. I went back to work when they were three months old, and Lucy was amazing with them."

"That must have been a very hard time for you," Lynette said sympathetically. "I met your husband a few times and he always seemed so nice. That's why I wanted to help with the scholarship."

Emma nodded. "Lynette secured several of our auction items for tonight. She can be very persuasive," she added with a wry smile.

"Anyway, I'm so glad you came tonight," Lynette continued to Renae. "I've been looking forward to meeting you. Our little gang gets together occasionally for dinner or game night. Maybe you'll come with Evan next time?"

It didn't escape Renae's notice that Lynette had basically invited her to come as Evan's companion rather than on her own. She suspected the implication had been unintentional, but it was a sign that Evan's friends were beginning to view them as a couple. Had he said anything to them about seeing her, or were they intuitive enough about their friend to have put the clues together? Knowing Evan, she suspected the latter was true.

"That sounds like fun," she said when she realized the others were waiting for some sort of response from her. "Maybe I will sometime."

"Oh, and feel free to bring the kids. Kim and Tate usually have Daryn with them, and she loves seeing other children," Lynette added.

This time Renae merely smiled. She wasn't sure how to explain that she'd been deliberately keeping Evan and her family apart. Emma gave her a look, but didn't say anything. Emma, of course, had seen that the kids didn't know Evan when they'd run into each other at the River Market.

"We also get together every Wednesday for lunch," Lynette rattled on.

"Yes, Evan told me about your lunches."

"You should join us sometime—especially before Emma leaves," Lynette added with a distinct pout.

"Lynette—"

"I know. Don't start." Lynette subsided with a sigh.

Having now met Emma's mother, a tiny, still-striking woman of Korean descent, Renae could understand why Emma didn't want discussion of her impending travel at the party. Just a passing mention of the upcoming assignment had Amy Grainger's eyes welling with tears she had bravely fought back, even though Emma had impatiently reminded her mother and everyone else within hearing that she wasn't moving to the other side of the world, and she had every intention of coming back home when the job was completed.

"I take it you've never lived away from your parents," Renae couldn't resist saying to Emma.

Tucking a strand of glossy dark hair behind her ear, Emma made a face. "I have my own apartment in Little Rock, but the farthest I've ever lived from them was when I went to college in Conway, a half hour drive from their house. They have their reasons for being so overprotective, but I just think it would be good for all of us for me to be completely independent. Besides, I'd like to see what else is out there, you know? I mean, I've traveled with my family and I went to Europe in college—but I've never truly lived on my own in a new place. I just want to see if I can do it."

"Aren't you nervous about it?" Lynette asked curiously, still resistant but looking more intrigued by Emma's explanation.

Emma laughed shortly. "I'm scared half to death. But I figure if I don't take a few risks I'll never know what I might have missed, you know?"

Renae felt her left eye twitch in what might have been a slight wince.

Evan and Tate rejoined them then, pleased that they'd just made a valuable business connection. From the front of the ballroom, Emma's dad announced that only five minutes remained before the close of the auction. Emma joined the ensuing, laughing rush toward the tables to make sure she was the final bidder on the afghan.

"Did you bid on anything?" Evan asked Renae with a smile.

"Of course. I left a bid on the dog training classes. Boomer could really benefit from that."

"Boomer, huh?" he asked with a chuckle. "This

would be the dog who caused you to fall off the step-ladder?"

She smiled up at him. "That would be the one."

He grinned. "Then yes, I would say lessons are definitely in order."

Their gazes locked for a moment, but then she looked away. Only to find herself meeting Lynette's indulgently approving smile. Lynette must have read more into that brief exchange than had actually been there, Renae assured herself.

She had told herself she wouldn't go up to Evan's apartment after the party, but would instead get straight into her car and head home. It wasn't very late when they drove into his parking lot, and she had no doubt she would be tempted to stay quite a while if she went upstairs.

Maybe he sensed her quandary. After turning off the engine, he gave her a moment before asking in a quiet voice, "Have you decided yet?"

She unfastened her seat belt. "Decided what?"

"Whether you're coming up. Surely you know I'm voting yes."

She yearned. That was the only word to describe the way she felt when she thought of entering Evan's apartment, moving into his arms. Though it had been only a week and a half since they'd made love, suddenly it felt so long. She'd suppressed the sensual side of her nature for a very long time, but now that Evan had reawakened it, it was hard to ignore.

Every time they were together, he became more important to her. Which admittedly terrified her.

If I don't take a few risks I'll never know what I might have missed, Emma had said.

Renae knew exactly what she would be missing. And she understood clearly the risks she faced.

With a sigh, she opened her purse and dug into it.

She sensed Evan's disapproval. "Looking for your keys?"

Taking out her phone, she peered down at the screen as she typed a quick message. "Just telling Lucy not to wait up for me."

He went still for a moment, then nodded in satisfaction. "Good."

Tiny white lights glimmering above her head and a low fire in the gas log fireplace were the only illumination in the deeply shadowed living room. Lying on a soft blanket spread on the floor, a snuggly fleece throw draped over her, Renae gazed up at the tree, mesmerized by the reflections on the shiny ornaments. Evan lay beside her, one arm beneath her, the other crooked behind his head.

Drawing her attention from the tree lights, she focused on Evan. He looked relaxed, contented. So very appealing. She reached out to trail a finger along his strong jaw.

He smiled at her. "What?"

She traced the curve of his lips. "Nothing."

He kissed her fingertip. "Okay."

"I have to leave soon."

His smile turned instantly to a frown. "Already?"

"It's getting late, Evan."

His sigh was both reluctant and resigned. "I know."

She sat up, holding the throw to her breasts and glancing toward the neat pile of clothing on the nearest chair.

Evan pushed himself upright beside her and ran a hand down her bare back. "It seems like you're always running off just as we're getting comfortable."

"A little too comfortable," she countered lightly, though his touch made her shiver. "Much longer and I'd have fallen asleep."

"I'd have been okay with that."

She turned her head to look at him. His knees drawn up in front of him, he rested his arms atop them, unselfconsciously nude. Not that he had any reason to be self-conscious—he looked like a statue of masculine perfection sitting there. She was conscious of her own imperfections—softness that could be a bit more toned, a few faded stretch marks from her pregnancy—but Evan never seemed to mind, or even notice, those flaws. Even now, he studied her with open admiration.

"You know I can't sleep here," she reminded him.

He nodded. "I know. But I still can't help thinking about how nice it would be to wake up with you."

It would be nice, she thought wistfully. But it wasn't going to happen. "I'm sure you're not used to seeing women who have to rush home to their kids after a rare free evening with you."

She wasn't sure why she'd spoken that thought aloud. Was she reminding Evan or herself of the reality that lay outside this firelit fantasy?

"This is a first for me," he admitted. "In a lot of ways."

She wasn't sure quite how to take that.

He leaned forward to kiss her shoulder. "I want more, Renae."

She swallowed hard in response to both the kiss and the husky murmur. "More what?"

"More than an occasional stolen hour. I want to see the other part of your life, too."

"There's nothing exciting about my life." Other than those stolen hours he'd mentioned, of course. "I go to work... I go home. I have dinner with my family, make lunches for myself and the kids. When I'm not at a school or church function with the family, I spend the evenings watching TV or playing board games with the kids and after they're in bed, I read or play gin rummy with Lucy. On weekends we shop or see G-rated movies or visit the zoo or a playground."

She spread her hand that wasn't holding the fleece throw. "With the exception of the occasional social or business function like tonight, Wednesday evening is the only time I'm completely on my own. And for the past couple of months, you've had those, so I'd say you know pretty much everything about me."

He had to have noticed how prominently Lucy figured into her life away from him. Had to understand the obstacles between them.

Still, he wasn't notably dissuaded. "It sounds like a good life."

"It has been," she admitted. Especially for the past couple of months, she added silently. Despite the doubts and anxiety he had caused her, these stolen hours with Evan had filled a gaping hole in her otherwise contented existence. The thought of how much she would miss these encounters when—not if—they ended filled her with dismay.

His hand slid down her back again. "I understand why you're reluctant to risk change. And I don't want to mess up a good thing. I'd just like to be a part of it. I know it's going to take a while for Lucy to come around, but maybe you and I could do something with the kids next weekend? Maybe we could take them to one of those pizza arcade places. Kids like those, don't they?"

"You, um, want to take the twins to an arcade?" She had a little trouble wrapping her head around that image.

"Your kids are such an important part of your life," he said simply. "I want to see that part, too."

She twisted a corner of the throw between her fingers. "I'm not sure it's such a good idea."

"Because of Lucy."

It wasn't really a question, but she shook her head, anyway. "No. Not entirely. It's just that I don't want to confuse the twins."

"You never take them out with your friends?" His question held a note of challenge.

"Well, yes, sometimes," she had to admit. "But—"

"You've already introduced me to them as your friend. Unless Lucy has told them something different about me?" he asked suspiciously.

"No. No, of course not."

Lucy would never tell the kids the basis for her hard feelings against Evan because she wouldn't want to upset them. She probably wouldn't pretend to like him, either, but she'd be tactfully vague about her reasons. At least in front of the twins. Renae, of course, would hear it all in detail again.

There was no doubt that Lucy would disapprove vehemently of Renae taking the children out with Evan. The question was, would Lucy be able to accept Renae's decisions without upsetting the happy balance in their little household? And did Evan have any idea what he was asking for in suggesting they take six-and-a-half-year-old twins to an arcade?

"Is it really that difficult a decision?" he asked, watching the expressions crossing her face.

Maybe it *would* be good for him to see that part of her life, she thought. As he'd pointed out, he had seen her only away from her real life and real responsibilities. Maybe it was time he saw for himself how different she was from the woman who could spend Wednesday evenings focusing solely on him.

Judging from her admittedly limited past experiences, reality would soon put a damper on romance. And maybe that would solve all her problems at once, one way or another.

"Fine."

He lifted his eyebrows in question. "Fine?"

"You want to spend an afternoon with the kids, we'll do it. Just remember it was your idea."

He seemed surprised that she had capitulated—as she was herself, a bit—but he adapted quickly enough. "Okay, great. Next Saturday?"

She nodded, thinking grimly of how crowded the pizza arcade would be on a Saturday afternoon this close to the holidays.

"What are you going to tell Lucy?"

"Let me worry about that." And she would worry. She reached for her clothes. "I really do have to go now."

Apparently satisfied with his small victory, he didn't try to detain her.

The blanket and throw were neatly folded and Evan was dressed when she returned from the bathroom. She knew he would walk her down to her car and see her safely away, even if she assured him he didn't need to go to the trouble.

He held out her coat to her with a smile that made her breath catch. It was both regretful and rueful, and so damned sexy-sweet that she couldn't look away. The smile faded in response to whatever he saw on her face.

"Renae—"

His husky murmur brought her out of her reverie. She shook her head to clear it and reached out to take her coat from his hand. "There's no need to walk me down."

He already had one arm in his own coat. "Mmm-hmm."

Which meant that he would, just as she had expected. She picked up her purse and pulled out her car keys.

Their breath hung in the air, mingling between them as they stood by her car to say good-night. "Be careful driving home," he said.

She nodded. "I will."

"Maybe you could tell the kids I said hi? I'd send greetings to Lucy, too, but I don't think she'd care to hear them."

"I'll tell them all you said hello," she assured him.

"Thanks."

"Good night, Evan."

He kissed her lingeringly. "I'll call you."

Nodding—and wondering what she'd gotten herself into now—she closed herself into her car and started the engine.

Renae waited until the kids were in bed Sunday night before sitting down with Lucy for a talk over tea in the kitchen. She'd been gearing up for this all day, and she

was as ready now as she would ever be for this over-
due discussion.

It had been a busy day. After church, the pastor and
his wife had joined them for a big lunch mostly prepared
by Lucy. The weather was cool but clear, so Renae had
taken the twins to a nearby playground that afternoon.
After dinner they'd made popcorn and watched a DVD.

After the film, the twins had gotten into a tugging
match over a toy they both wanted to play with, which
had almost ended the otherwise pleasant day with them
being sent to bed early as a consequence. Fortunately,
they had gotten themselves under control and grudgingly apologized to each other beneath their mother's
stern gaze. They'd gone to bed an hour later with the
usual hugs and kisses and giggles, the quarrel forgotten. Renae hadn't tried to fool herself that it would be
the last one—her children were generally well behaved,
but they had their moments.

She hoped they wouldn't have any of those "moments" at the arcade next weekend.

She hadn't told them yet that they would be going on
that outing. First she had to talk to Lucy.

She took a sip of her tea, then set the cup on the table,
cradling it loosely between her hands. "We haven't had
a chance to talk about the party last night."

Lucy lowered her own cup, looking over the top of
her narrow, gold-framed glasses at Renae. "No, we
haven't. Did you have a nice time?"

"Yes, it was very nice. The auction was a success.
They raised quite a bit for the charities, so the scholarship fund should get a nice little boost."

"I'm happy to hear that."

"I bid on doggie obedience classes, but I got outbid."

Lucy gave a faint chuckle. "Those might have come in handy."

"We'll probably enroll him after the first of the year, anyway. You'll be happy to know that your afghan went to a good home. Emma Grainger bought it. She absolutely loves it."

"That's the young woman we met at the River Market? Evan Daugherty's girlfriend?"

"Yes, we met her, but she isn't Evan's girlfriend. They're just friends."

"Good for her. She seemed nice." *Too nice for Evan,* she might as well have added.

Renae resisted a sigh. "She is nice. I enjoyed spending time with her last night."

"I figured you were having a good time when you got home so late. Guess the party went on longer than you expected?"

Drawing a deep breath, Renae put her hands in her lap and laced her fingers together. It was ridiculous that she felt like a teenager making a confession to her mother—at least, this was the way she assumed she would feel in that situation she had never actually experienced. "I wasn't actually at the party the whole evening. I spent some time visiting with Evan afterward."

She didn't know if her mother-in-law would figure out that she'd used *visiting* as a euphemism, but that was as much detail as Renae was willing to give on that count.

Whether she'd caught the nuance or not, Lucy stiffened hard enough to make her chair creak a little. "Just you and him?"

"Yes. I've seen him several times recently, Lucy. I

didn't mention it because I knew you'd disapprove, but I don't want to hide it from you any longer."

Lucy clung a bit longer to her shaky optimism. "I know you've been meeting him about the scholarship. Is that what you were talking about last night?"

"No. We have taken care of the scholarship, but we've also been meeting socially. I, um, guess you would call it dating."

Blinking rapidly, Lucy asked in little more than a whisper, "You're dating Evan Daugherty?"

That seemed like the easiest way to explain it. "Yes. It's all still tentative, and I don't know where it's headed, but I'm going to keep seeing him. For now."

"I can't believe this…"

"I don't want to upset you, Lucy," Renae said softly. "And I truly don't want to hurt you. I didn't plan this… it just sort of happened."

A glint of anger sparked in Lucy's dark eyes, but it wasn't aimed at Renae. "He talked you into this, didn't he? I knew there was a reason he reappeared in your life."

"It really was just a coincidence that he came to the office," Renae insisted. "And I was the one who asked to be involved with the scholarship."

"He convinced you to hide it from me. Why else wouldn't you have told me before?"

"No, that was my decision, too. I just—didn't know how to tell you. I'm sorry."

Predictably, Lucy wasn't appeased. "I've always suspected he had an eye on you. Even when my Jason was alive, I thought Evan looked at you too much."

That stung, maybe because it hit a little too close to home.

"There was never anything between Evan and me when Jason and I were together, Lucy." Not beyond one brief kiss and a barely acknowledged attraction. She refused to concede that added up to wrongdoing, no matter how much guilt she'd felt afterward.

Lucy waved a hand. "I know you would never have been unfaithful to my Jason. But I don't trust Evan Daugherty. Never have."

"Yes, you've made that clear." Frankly, Renae was getting tired of hearing it.

"I've had good reason. Did I tell you about the time he got my son arrested?"

It was another old story Renae had heard several times. Evan and Jason, along with several other high school boys, had been hauled down to the police station after a big fight on campus. "I know about that, but—"

"Evan threw the first punch," Lucy said with a firm nod of her head. "He even admitted it."

And Jason had told Renae why that punch had been thrown. Evan, Jason and another friend had come upon a group of bullies tormenting a younger student. A pushing match had begun, followed by ugly words that had pushed Evan's temper beyond the boiling point. He'd punched the bully, which had sparked a full-out melee that had been broken up by the campus security officer. No charges had been filed, but all the boys involved had received stern warnings and several Saturday detention sessions at school.

"Evan said later he was sorry he'd hit the guy, but I always thought he was totally justified," Jason had confided to Renae. "The jerk deserved it."

Lucy was in no mood now to hear a defense of Evan's actions, even in her late son's own words.

"That was a long time ago, Lucy," Renae said instead.

"It was just one of the troubles Evan caused this family. And you know the worst." Lucy dabbed at her eyes with a paper napkin.

This was what Renae had feared—that Lucy would cry. She had a hard time dealing with her mother-in-law's tears.

She reached across the table and covered Lucy's hand with her own. "Lucy, Evan didn't kill Jason. All he did was invite him for a ride on their bikes. Jason wanted to go. All the blame goes to Sam Abbott."

Abbott was the man who had been driving the car that hit Jason. He was still serving time for manslaughter as a result, having pleaded guilty to avoid a trial and a potentially longer sentence than the one he'd received. While Renae and Lucy hadn't been happy that Abbott had not received the maximum sentence allowable because of his plea deal, they'd both been relieved to be spared the trial.

Renae had no doubt Abbott's lawyers had convinced the man that his previous history of reckless driving combined with the image of a grieving mother and young, pregnant widow would have persuaded any jury to want to put him away for life. There had been a civil settlement, but because Abbott had no insurance and had declared personal bankruptcy, Renae never expected to see a dime of it.

Lucy hated Sam Abbott, of course, but at least that hostility was rational.

Lucy met her eyes. "You know how I feel about this, Renae."

"Yes." Renae drew a deep breath. "And I'm sorry. But I'm not going to stop seeing Evan."

Lucy flinched. Had she really thought Renae would cave so easily? Maybe Renae had gotten too much into the habit of looking after everyone else's happiness, which left others expecting her to continue to do so.

"I loved Jason," she said. "I married him thinking I would spend my entire life with him. But he's been gone a long time and I'm not ready to join Daisy and Maxine for dominoes on Thursday nights."

Lucy released a long sigh. "I know you're still young. You gave up your entire twenties to take care of the children and to make a home for them—and me."

"We've done that together, Lucy."

"Yes, but maybe I've held you back in starting a new life for yourself. Just because I never looked to remarry after my Luis died doesn't mean you wanted to spend the rest of your life alone. I must confess it's difficult for me to imagine you with anyone other than Jason, but you shouldn't worry about that."

Taking encouragement from that, Renae started to speak, but Lucy beat her to it.

"What about that nice man with the little boys? Mike? He's interested in you. I'm sure he would ask you out if you gave him a little encouragement."

"I'm not interested in going out with Mike."

"There's that man from church. Winn Kiplinger, the one who lost his wife last year? He's a few years older than you, but—"

"Lucy," Renae cut in with exasperation. "I don't need you to start matchmaking. I'm not planning to remarry anytime soon. I just wanted you to know that I've been spending time with Evan and that I'll be seeing him again. I'd like for you to give him another chance to be friendly with you, but if you'd rather not see him, that's fine, too."

Her expression set, Lucy muttered, "I have no interest in being friendly with him. It's just too painful."

Renae gave up. Now that they had finally gotten this talk started, she wouldn't push Lucy any further on that count tonight. Maybe Lucy would come around—or maybe things with Evan would end before that became necessary. For now, all Renae could do was take this one day at a time.

There was still one last hurdle to cross before the conversation ended. "You should know that Evan and I are taking the kids to a pizza arcade next Saturday."

Lucy looked horrified. "You're taking the twins out with him? Why?"

"Because Evan wants to get to know them. He can't really understand my life without seeing me with my children."

Lucy clattered dishes irritably as she gathered her teacup and dessert plate to carry to the kitchen. "I don't think that's a good idea. That man is too persuasive. Think how susceptible Daniel would be to him. Do you know how awful it will be if they grow fond of him only to be hurt by him? As they probably will be," she added in an ominous tone.

Hearing her own fear put into words, Renae cleared her throat. "I'll be careful with them. And really, that would be a risk no matter who I see—even Mike Bishop or Winn Kiplinger," she added meaningfully. "So, either I never have another date until the twins are grown, or teach them to appreciate the people who come through our lives. Even if only temporarily."

Standing by the table and wringing her hands, Lucy fretted. "I don't like this. I don't like this at all."

"I know. And I'm sorry." But Renae wasn't going to change her mind. As far as she was concerned, this talk had only reinforced how set in their ways she and Lucy had become, and how it was past time for her to shake things up a bit.

She could only hope the path she was taking now didn't lead straight from happiness to heartbreak.

Evan took Renae to dinner with Tate and Kim Wednesday night. It had been a spur-of-the-moment plan cooked up between Evan and Tate during work Tuesday, but Renae and Kim had approved. They had burgers the guys cooked on an outdoor grill, and roasted potatoes and salad the women prepared together while little Daryn watched happily from her high chair.

It was cool out that night, and both Evan and Tate were red-cheeked and windblown by the time they carried in the platter of burgers, but Evan figured the appreciation they received made it worth the discomfort. They talked easily over dinner, laughing at Daryn, who serenaded them with a wooden-spoon drum solo on her high-chair tray, enjoying the extra attention she was receiving.

Kim and Renae insisted on cleaning the kitchen after dinner, leaving the baby in the living room with the men. Bouncing a chortling Daryn on his knee, Evan decided he was getting better at interacting with his partner's little stepdaughter—daughter, he corrected himself. Tate planned to adopt Daryn as soon as legally possible and Evan had no doubt Tate would forever love the girl as much as he would any biological offspring.

Tate glanced toward the kitchen. "Kim and Renae seem to be getting along well. They have a lot in common, I guess."

Evan passed the baby to Tate. "Yes, they do."

Tickling Daryn's chin to make her squeal with delight, Tate asked, "So is Lucy coming around?"

Evan grimaced. "Renae said Lucy just doesn't mention me at all. Even this morning, knowing Renae and I would be seeing each other this evening, she just told her she would see her at the usual Wednesday night time and acted like nothing had changed."

He knew that because he'd pressed Renae a little for the details when she'd been reticent about Lucy. He needed to know what he was up against in the six days a week he and Renae were apart. He figured Lucy would do everything in her power to undermine the advances he and Renae were slowly making.

"Got to be tough for Renae. Caught in the middle that way, I mean."

"I know." Which was why he was doing his best not to make things worse for her even as he pushed to be included more in her life.

"So are y'all still taking her kids to the arcade Saturday?"

"Yes."

"Have you ever actually been to one of those places?"

"Well…no. But I've heard about them. Pizza and games, right? I can play some Skee-Ball with the kids."

"Mmm." Tate gave him a look that might have held a hint of sympathy.

Evan pushed himself to his feet. "I think I need some more iced tea. Want me to bring you a glass?"

Tate tossed Daryn a few inches in the air, catching her on a fit of giggles. "Yeah, sure, thanks."

Carrying their empty glasses for the refills, Evan moved toward the kitchen. He heard the women talking as he approached, and he couldn't help overhearing what they were saying. He held back a minute before entering, not wanting to interrupt.

"Tate is so cute with Daryn," Renae remarked. "It's obvious that she adores him. And vice versa."

"You should have seen him when he first met her," Kim confided in amusement. "He was terrified of her. So afraid he would do something wrong with her. He'd never been around babies much before."

"He's obviously gotten over that."

Kim chuckled. "You could say he had an immersion course in child care. Daryn and I were sick and he had to take care of her on his own for a couple of days. We're talking feverish, cranky baby with nausea and toxic diapers. And I couldn't even crawl out of bed to help him."

"Wow. That would be a challenge for anyone."

"He handled it beautifully. And oddly enough—" Kim's soft laugh held lingering incredulity "—he asked me to marry him that very weekend."

Realizing abruptly that he was eavesdropping, Evan started forward. He stopped abruptly when he heard Renae say, "Tate's one of a rare breed then. Seems like a lot of men like the thrill of a new romance, but they find the day-to-day grind of marriage and kids too repetitive and restrictive."

"Ouch. Sounds like you're quoting. Bad dates?"

"Something like that."

Evan clinked the glasses together lightly then stepped

through the doorway, saying as he entered, "Any more of that iced tea? Tate and I worked up a thirst out there."

Kim moved immediately toward the fridge. Renae gave Evan a sharp look, which he met with a bland smile.

"You should come out here and see Daryn get across the living room," he advised her. "She's only been crawling for a month or so and she's already starting to pull up on furniture. Cute as a little button. I'm betting Tate she'll be full-out running in another month."

Filling the tea glasses, Kim groaned heartily. "You guys and your bets."

Evan smiled, unable to stop thinking about the things Renae had said.

Had she been talking about him? Or thinking back to Jason's preparenthood cold feet?

What would it take to prove to her that he was fully prepared for the challenges inherent in joining a ready-made family?

Chapter Ten

Though he had thought himself prepared for the experience, Evan was overwhelmed by the sheer chaos of the arcade. Shouldn't there be a limit on how many kids were allowed in one building? Because he figured there were almost enough to make the walls of the place bulge out—or maybe that was just the impression he got from the running, squealing, laughing, pushing and crying kids that were everywhere he looked.

"You did ask for this," Renae reminded him after the first deafening fifteen minutes. She'd had to raise her voice to be heard over the din of children, bells, whistles and buzzers all underscored by shrill-voiced kiddie songs piped from hidden speakers.

"Yeah," he said with a nod, watching the twins crawling through a clear plastic tunnel over his head. "It's…interesting."

Most of a pizza sat abandoned on the booth table where they had sat rather briefly after arriving. The bland pie hadn't really appealed to Evan nor, apparently, to Renae. The kids seemed to like it okay, but they were much more interested in playing than eating.

They had accepted Evan's presence with remarkable aplomb, considering they had met him only once before. They'd chattered away as if they knew him well, proving that both had inherited their father's gregariousness. He'd kept up pretty well, though they tended to drop names of their friends and neighbors as if he was supposed to know everyone they did. Occasionally Renae supplied some information for him, but mostly she simply held back and left him to interact with them on his own.

A test, perhaps? If so, he thought he was doing pretty well so far.

He'd picked them up at their house. Lucy had been nowhere to be seen—he was quite sure she'd made a point to be gone when he arrived—but he hadn't said a word about that. Renae had made sure the kids were safely strapped into the backseat of the pickup, and then he'd driven them all straight here.

Disentangled from the tunnel, the twins ran toward them. "Want to play air hockey with me, Evan?" Daniel asked. Though Renae had initially suggested that the kids should call him Mr. Daugherty, Evan had urged them to use his first name instead. "I'm pretty good."

"Sure," he said, making a mental note to let the kid win. "Show me your skills."

The kid slaughtered him. Rather than generously throwing the game, Evan had to make an effort just to score a couple of points. He blamed it on the many distractions around him. Besides which, the kid was fast.

"That's okay, Evan," Leslie consoled him afterward. "Daniel always wins air hockey. You should play Skee-Ball with him. He's not as good at that."

Evan and Renae exchanged an amused glance over the girl's head.

They played Skee-Ball. And video games and Whac-A-Mole and a couple of other games he couldn't identify. He was nearly mowed down a couple of times by oblivious kids, and had pizza sauce smeared down the leg of his jeans by a runaway toddler. His head was starting to hurt.

Renae was different with the kids. He'd figured she would be, but still he found the changes striking. Even when she was talking to Evan, her attention was focused on her kids. She knew where they were and what they were doing at all times, and she had a way of communicating with them without words, letting them know when to settle down or be more careful, stopping a couple of potential quarrels with only a stern look. She cheered them on and high-fived them when they played well. And when Leslie was pushed down by a girl racing her to a game they both wanted to play, Renae gave her daughter a hug and stopped her tears by leading her to another game they could play together. Evan was tempted to give the other girl a piece of his mind, but Renae stopped him with a calming hand on his arm.

She was very…motherly, he decided. In comparison to the woman who'd made love with him beneath his tree, the difference was a bit unsettling. But was he as attracted to her now as he had been then?

He watched as Leslie clapped her hands with a squeal

when bells rang and a light flashed and a long ribbon of prize tickets spat out from a slot on a machine. Looking almost as excited as the child, Renae hugged her daughter tightly, giving Evan a bright smile over Leslie's head. His stomach tightened.

Oh, yeah. Definitely still attracted.

It was time he stopped fighting it and started chipping away at the barriers that had been troubling them both so far.

Renae had to give Evan credit for effort. He had survived the past ninety minutes with remarkable aplomb, considering it was glaringly obvious he had little to no experience with kiddie arcades. He even remained outwardly patient while the twins dithered for what seemed like an eternity over the cheap trinkets for which they wanted to trade their prize tickets.

Leslie, especially, had a hard time deciding between a glittery plastic bracelet and a cheap-looking stuffed unicorn. She spent so long debating that Daniel, his hands full of his own carefully chosen awards, grew impatient and began to nag at her to hurry up. Leslie snapped back at him, which caused him to snarl a response.

Tears and anger threatened when Renae interceded quickly. "Daniel, leave your sister alone. Leslie, you have two minutes to make your choice or we're going to have to leave without either."

"Can't I just pay for one of them?" Evan asked her in a low voice. "I mean, those things can't cost this place more than a buck apiece, if that."

Renae wasn't sure if he'd made the offer because

he wanted Leslie to have both toys or because he was past ready to get out of the place. She shook her head.

"She needs to learn to make choices, and that she can't have everything she wants," she explained in a murmur. "One minute, Leslie."

A few minutes later, they walked out to Evan's truck. Tired, overstimulated and still looking a bit pouty, Leslie carried the stuffed unicorn. Evan opened the back passenger door for the girl.

"I like the unicorn better," he assured her. "The bracelet was kind of gaudy."

Preparing to climb into the high vehicle, Leslie paused to look up at him doubtfully. "You like the unicorn?"

"Yeah, that's the one I'd have picked. What are you going to name it?"

"Peaches," Leslie replied without hesitation.

"Oh." Evan blinked. "Sure, that's a great name for a unicorn."

He boosted her into the seat, then stepped back to let Renae check the seat-belt buckle. She noted that Leslie was smiling now, and playing with the unicorn with a new appreciation.

Daniel had climbed into his side of the truck without assistance. "Do you like my dinosaurs, Evan? They're cool, huh?"

"Very," Evan assured him, looking around from the driver's seat to admire the six-inch-tall plastic figures. "I especially like the velociraptor, though the stegosaurus is pretty cool, too."

Daniel looked suitably impressed that Evan had correctly identified the plastic creatures. "Yeah. Look, they're fighting. Rowr, rowr."

He clashed the two figures together, providing noisy sound effects for the battle. Renae gave him some leeway until he attacked his sister's unicorn with the velociraptor, eliciting a yelp of protest from her.

"That's enough, Daniel. Leave Leslie alone and play quietly until we get home."

It wasn't a long drive. Remembering that Lucy had said she would be spending that evening at the church decorating for an upcoming Christmas pageant, Renae invited Evan in for coffee. It seemed only polite to do so, and he accepted immediately.

While she made the coffee, the twins insisted on showing Evan their Christmas tree with the growing stack of wrapped presents beneath, their rooms and toys, and their backyard swing set. Excited by having someone new to admire him, Boomer yapped and bounced around their feet, wagging frantically when Evan rubbed his ears. Daniel was almost as demanding of Evan's attention as his puppy.

She sent the children off to play while she and Evan drank their coffee in the kitchen. Though he didn't actually say so, she suspected he appreciated the peace that fell over the room.

"It was your idea," she reminded him with a slight smile.

"I know. It's been…interesting."

She was amused by his choice of adjective. "I'm sure it has."

"You've got good kids, Renae. Compared to some of those little monsters at the arcade, yours are almost angels."

She laughed wryly. "Not quite, but thank you. Lucy

and I have worked hard to instill good manners in them."

"Um. Yeah. Where is she, anyway?"

"She's working at the church this evening. Her Sunday school class planned to have dinner out, then decorate for the Christmas pageant this week. Which, by the way, is Wednesday evening, so I won't be able to see you then. The kids are in the pageant."

He nodded, looking at her steadily across the table. Was he waiting for an invitation? Though she knew she should extend one, she bit her lip, the words trapped inside her.

"I'll miss seeing you," he said when her silence continued.

"I'll miss you, too," she admitted with a sigh.

Those simple statements were hardly earthshaking, but she sensed their significance. They were becoming entangled in each other's lives in more ways than the no-strings fling she had initially thought she was entering into. Introducing him to her children was a huge step. Integrating him into family holiday traditions with Lucy was much more problematic. And perhaps way too soon.

A burst of childish laughter came from another part of the house. Renae cocked her head to listen, but relaxed when she decided the kids were just playing in the living room. She looked back at Evan, noting that he was watching her closely. Was he aware that her attention was always divided when her children were nearby?

"Is there any other evening this week when you'd be free to see me?" he asked.

She hesitated, thinking of the busy weeks ahead. "It's going to be pretty hectic around here between now and

Christmas. The kids are out of school after next week. They have several parties to attend, and I have a few functions, myself—my office Christmas party and a baby shower for one of my friends."

Evan was frowning now. "You're saying we can't see each other again until after Christmas?"

"I didn't say that, exactly," she murmured. "I just said it's going to be a little tricky finding extra time."

"Well, let me know when you find a few minutes to work me in."

She supposed she couldn't blame him for sounding peevish—she was sure he was busy, too. Still, she added, "You knew about my obligations when we started this, Evan."

He nodded somewhat grimly. "I'm not trying to make your life any more difficult. I just want to be with you when we can."

"I know." He had complicated her life, but not entirely in a bad way, she mused, softening. And he had been very patient with her when she'd stalled and dithered about their relationship in much the same way her daughter had deliberated over arcade prizes.

Leslie skipped through the kitchen door, a book in her arms. She plopped it down open in front of Evan and pointed with one chubby finger. "This is you and my daddy."

Renae hadn't expected Leslie to unearth the photo album, and Evan obviously hadn't, either. He looked at Renae for a moment, then almost reluctantly turned his attention to the photograph. His smile was a little strained when he spoke to Leslie. "Yes, that's right. That's an old picture. My hair looked pretty funny then, didn't it?"

"It was kind of long," Leslie agreed solemnly. "But you look the same 'cept for that."

"You think so, huh?"

Leslie nodded. "You were my daddy's friend."

"Yes, I was."

Twisting a dark strand of hair around one finger, Leslie gazed up at him. "I didn't know him. But my Grammy says he was special."

"He was special," Evan assured her a bit huskily. "And he would have loved you and your brother very much."

"Grammy says that, too."

"Take the album back to my room now, Leslie," Renae said, her throat tight.

"Yes, ma'am." Leslie picked up the book, then hesitated, still looking at Evan. "We're having a Christmas pageant at our church this week."

Evan shot a look at Renae before nodding. "Yes, I heard."

"Daniel's going to be a shepherd boy and I'm an angel."

Chuckling, Evan reached out to run a hand lightly over Leslie's hair. "Perfect casting."

Sensing what was coming, Renae braced herself, unsure how to stop it.

"Maybe you could come watch us?" Leslie asked Evan innocently. "They told us to ask all our friends."

"I'm glad you consider me a friend. I'll have to check my calendar about the pageant—I'm not sure I'll be free that night. I know you and Daniel will be the stars of the program, though."

"Okay. I hope you can come." Leslie dashed out of the room again with the album.

Evan stood abruptly, his chair scraping on the tile floor. He carried his coffee cup to the sink, setting it on the counter. "I'd better go before Lucy gets home."

Renae drew a deep breath and rose to her feet. "Evan? I'd like you to come to the pageant, too."

His eyes narrowed as he frowned down at her. "You would?"

"Yes."

"What about Lucy?"

She ran her hands over the front of her jeans. "I'll talk to her."

Stepping forward, Evan rested his hands on her shoulders, gazing down at her with an intensity that unnerved her a little. "I told you I don't want to complicate your life. I meant that. I really appreciate you asking me to join you, but I won't ruin your evening with Lucy and the kids."

"I said I would talk to her. She won't like it, but there's not a lot she can do about it."

He hesitated only a second, then shook his head with a sigh. "I would never ask you to choose between me and Lucy, Renae. For one thing, I know that ultimately, I would lose," he said with a faint smile of resignation. "But mostly, it just wouldn't be fair to you. She's your family, your children's grandmother. Maybe I don't quite understand the arrangement you have, but I would never do anything to put a strain on your relationship with her."

She swallowed a lump in her throat. "Thank you."

"Things will settle down after the holidays, and in the meantime, I'll see you when you have an available hour or two, okay?"

She reached up with her right hand to cover his left. "I really would like to have you there."

"I believe you." He brushed a chaste kiss across her forehead. "And I'd like to be there. Maybe in the future, I will be. But this time, I'd better pass. Give the kids my regrets, will you?"

Very aware of his mention of the future, she nodded. "I will."

It would have been easy to believe that Evan had used Lucy as an excuse not to come to the church pageant, Renae thought as she watched him drive away after he said goodbye to the twins. The thing was, she thought he would really have liked to be there. Even after what had to have been a fairly miserable afternoon for him at the arcade, he was still trying to be a part of her life— and not just in bed.

Would it be completely reckless and irresponsible of her to hope that this wasn't just physical after all?

Or had she unwittingly done that from the start?

Between the last-of-the-year rush at work and the chaos of the holidays and the underlying tension at home, Renae felt drawn in a half-dozen different directions. Evan hadn't been making demands on her, but she wanted to be with him, too. There were only two situations in which she'd felt truly at peace during the past two weeks—when she snuggled with her children reading bedtime stories and when she lay in Evan's arms on the rare occasion she could be with him.

On the Friday evening before Christmas, she and Evan nestled on his couch, her head on his shoulder, his arms around her. Lucy was at home with the kids, probably pretending Renae wasn't with Evan.

It was only the second time Renae and Evan had managed to be alone since the arcade outing, though they had taken the kids for ice cream earlier that afternoon. Both Renae and Evan had taken the afternoon off work for the upcoming holiday weekend, taking advantage of the time to be together. Evan had given the twins Christmas gifts during the outing, since he wouldn't see them again before the holiday. He'd been overly generous and needless to say, the kids had been thrilled.

She wished she could say the same about Lucy. When Renae had taken the kids home, the twins had shown Lucy their gifts, expecting her to be as delighted as they were. Instead, she had merely nodded and said coolly, "Yes, very nice."

Because she had undoubtedly known Renae would be angry, Lucy had said nothing negative about Evan in front of the kids. But the twins were more perceptive than she gave them credit for.

"Why doesn't Grammy like Evan?" Leslie had asked Renae in confusion after Lucy made an excuse to leave the room. "I asked her, but she said I shouldn't worry about it and then she looked sad."

"I like Evan," Daniel had insisted from the floor where he played with the dinosaur building-block set Evan had given him. He was already in the process of building an impressive tyrannosaurus rex to battle the two plastic dinosaurs that waited nearby. "Grammy would, too, if she'd get to know him."

Renae had drawn a deep breath. "Grammy gets sad because Evan was your daddy's friend and he reminds her of how much she misses your daddy. Just give her a little time. She'll come around."

It had been a rather vague response, but the best she

could do at the time. It was hard to convince the kids that things would change when she wasn't sure if Lucy would ever accept Evan—or if Evan would stay around long enough for her to get to that point.

She sighed.

His cheek resting on her head, Evan asked, "What's wrong?"

"Nothing. I was just thinking."

"The kids seemed to have a good time this afternoon."

"They had a ball. They loved their gifts from you."

"I'm glad. I have one for you, too, you know."

He reached beneath the tree and handed her a pretty, gold-wrapped package. Somewhat shyly, she dug into her big bag on the floor, and pulled out a gift for him. She had spent hours deliberating over it, and she hoped he would like what she'd chosen. "I have one for you, too."

Sitting side by side, they opened their gifts at the same time. Renae loved the gold bracelet nestled in a midnight-blue velvet box. She thought of protesting that he'd spent too much, but that seemed ungracious. "Evan, this is beautiful."

"I hope you like it. I know you don't wear a lot of jewelry, but I saw it when I was shopping for my sister and I thought it was nice."

"It's lovely."

She watched a bit nervously as he opened the box holding the gift she had purchased for him.

"It's a wooden pen." He lifted the implement from the cotton-lined box with care. "Wow, this is beautiful, Renae."

"It's hand-turned by a local woodworking artist,"

she informed him. "I bought it at the museum store downtown."

He twisted the mechanism to reveal the rollerball point. "It's great. What's the wood?"

"It's curly maple, made from Arkansas wood. It made me think of you, for some reason."

"It's perfect," he assured her. "I'll carry it with pride. Thank you."

He leaned over to kiss her, an embrace that lingered quite a long time.

Somehow that exchange of gifts made their relationship seem even more serious.

Eventually she had to go. He walked her down to her car, where they shared several more kisses before he reluctantly opened her car door for her.

"Have a wonderful Christmas with your family," she told him, reaching up to touch his face.

He caught her hand and pressed a kiss in her palm. "You, too."

"I'm sure I will." But she would miss him, she thought as she drove slowly home. Even though they had never shared a Christmas together, she knew she would miss having him there.

Chapter Eleven

"Why can't we have Evan over for dinner?" Daniel demanded almost a month into the new year. "We always go somewhere to see him, and he never gets to come here. I still haven't showed him all the stuff Santa brought me."

"Me, neither," Leslie seconded from her place at the dinner table. "Evan would like your cooking, Grammy. We should ask him for dinner."

Renae figured if Lucy's face tightened any further it would be in danger of cracking. "Maybe we will sometime. Are you two finished with your desserts? If so, carry your plates into the kitchen. Weren't you going to play with that new video game you got for Christmas? Your mother said you could play for an hour after dinner."

It was a blatant redirection of their attention, of

course, but it worked. The twins hurriedly finished their puddings and carried their dishes into the kitchen, then raced to the living room to play the new game.

"I hope you're satisfied," Lucy said, turning immediately to Renae. "Those children are going to have their little hearts broken, just like you are. I did everything I knew how to convince you to protect them, but you wouldn't listen."

"Please don't start this again, Lucy."

They had maintained an uneasy truce about Evan for the past month, with Lucy stubbornly refusing to mention him and Renae trying to appease her by keeping her interactions with Evan separate from her life with Lucy. She had continued to see him on Wednesday evenings and occasionally took the kids to meet him somewhere on the weekends. But despite the steps she had taken to keep her mother-in-law appeased, she wouldn't let Lucy criticize her maternal decisions. "Evan is not going to hurt the kids."

"They're getting fond of him. Trying to bring him into our family. How will they feel if it doesn't work between you two?"

"You and I have had this talk. If Evan drifts away, I'll encourage the twins to hold on to fond memories of the time we spent with him. They'll be fine."

"If all they do is go for pizza with him, perhaps, but if they start seeing him as a member of the family and then he disappears?"

Renae groaned. "All they want to do is ask him to dinner, Lucy. And I think it's a good idea. The children accept Evan as my friend, and the four of us enjoy spending time together. I would like for you to join us."

She held up a hand before her mother-in-law could

speak. "I won't ask you to cook for him. I'll take care of that. All I ask is that you dine with us. You barely have to speak to him, though I would hope you'd be polite in front of the twins."

Lucy grumbled.

Renae softened her voice. "I know it's painful for you to see him, Lucy. He's still here and Jason isn't. But holding on to this anger is only hurting you."

Lucy sighed shakily and shoved her chair back from the table. "Fine. Invite him for dinner. We'll see how long he stays around when he sees how busy and ordinary your life is normally."

That struck a little too close to Renae's own secret concerns. Maybe it also explained her sudden decision to bring Evan into her home, she mused, fingering the bracelet on her right wrist. As close as she had been getting to him during the past weeks, maybe it was time to find out just how committed he was.

Because if it's going to end, she thought, *it'll be easier now than later—for everyone involved.*

Renae wouldn't have called Friday night's dinner a disaster. But it was hardly a glowing success, either. The twins were overly excited and competed fiercely for Evan's attention. After greeting Evan with a cool courtesy she would have displayed toward a total stranger, Lucy responded to anything he said with such excruciating politeness that Renae could almost see him wince.

After dinner, Daniel all but dragged Evan into the living room to play a video game. Lucy sat on the couch, her knitting needles clicking sharply as she watched them with an intensity that obviously made Evan uncomfortable.

She walked him out to his car after dinner. It was cold, and she huddled into her coat, pulling her collar up to shield her neck. Her breath was a ghostly cloud in the pale security lighting. "I'm sorry about the way Lucy acted tonight."

He chuckled, though without much humor. "She was perfectly polite."

"Yes, I noticed," Renae said dryly.

He shrugged. "It's okay. I wasn't expecting her to welcome me with open arms."

"The kids were pretty hyper tonight, too. Daniel kept begging you to play that game again whenever you tried to stop."

"I had a good time playing with Daniel. And before you apologize for them, too, I didn't mind letting Leslie read me a book or rubbing Boomer's ears."

She drew her coat more snugly around her. "I'm sure that's not the way you're accustomed to spending your evenings."

"No," he admitted. "I'm accustomed to spending my evenings sitting on the couch by myself in front of the TV and wishing you were there with me."

That didn't encourage her. "But I can only be there one night a week, occasionally two. And when you come here, you have to run the gamut of Lucy's dirty looks and the kids and the dog climbing all over you, and you and I barely have time to exchange a few words."

"That will surely get better once everyone's used to having me around."

"I can't blame you if you aren't in any hurry to repeat the experience," she said, thinking that despite what he said, he must have more interesting ways to spend his time.

"If tonight was a test, I think I passed," he said, an edge to his voice. "I'm not running, Renae. I'm not looking for excuses to avoid future family dinners. I'm not even angry with your mother-in-law for doing everything she can to sabotage this relationship. Frustrated, maybe, but not angry. I don't scare off that easily."

"It wasn't a test," Renae muttered, noting his use of the relationship word.

"Maybe it's time you start having a little faith in me, Renae. I knew when we started seeing each other that you have obligations. Your kids, your job, your mother-in-law who would be perfectly happy for everything to stay exactly the same for the rest of her life. If all I wanted was an easy affair, I'd be content with the occasional Wednesday evening with you. Maybe that *was* all I wanted, at first. But maybe you've noticed I'm the one who's been pushing for more lately."

She bit her lip.

He stroked his thumb across her mouth, easing her lip from between her teeth. "I'm not going anywhere, Renae. Not unless you've grown tired of me. In that case, I'll stay away."

Her long sigh was visible in the air between them. "I don't want you to stay away. I just—"

—don't know why you want to keep coming back, she completed silently.

The kiss he gave her then was partially an answer. He drew back slowly, smiling down at her in a way that revealed little of his thoughts. "Thanks for dinner. I'll call you tomorrow."

She lifted a hand in a wave as his truck disappeared from sight. Only then did she turn back toward the house. Her hands deep in the pockets of her coat, she

stood for a moment studying the lighted windows behind which waited her family.

Maybe Lucy wasn't the only one who had been clinging to the status quo. The question was, how could she
make sure the changes she made would make their lives
better? Renae knew there were no guarantees in life—
but when she was being pulled in so many directions,
it would be nice to have some sort of sign about what
would bring the least chance of disappointment. For
all of them.

It didn't snow often in Central Arkansas. Once,
sometimes twice in a winter, they would see measur-
able accumulation, generally less than four inches.
When snow did cover the ground, most activity in the
area ground to a halt because of lack of snow removal
equipment. Grocery shelves emptied, schools closed,
even many businesses closed for a day or two until the
snow melted.

The twins were delighted to wake up on the last
Friday morning in January to find the ground hidden
beneath a rare blanket of snow, with more still falling.
Up to six inches were predicted to accumulate by the
end of the day. Renae didn't even have to check the local
morning news to know that school was dismissed, but
it was habit to tune in. The snowfall was the leading
story that morning with school closings running con-
tinuously across the bottom of the screen.

Her phone rang early with a call from Ann to inform
her that there was no need for her to come to work that
day. "Stay home with your kids," she urged. "We're not
expecting many patients to show up today anyway, and
there's nothing that can't wait until Monday. Cathy lives

close enough to get to the office easily and she said she can handle the desk today."

Because she hadn't been looking forward to slipping and sliding her way across the river along with the other local drivers who had little experience with snow, Renae accepted the offer gratefully.

"Looks like we'll all be home today," she said, setting her phone aside.

The twins did celebratory dances at the breakfast table while Lucy turned from the stove and smiled. "Yay!" Leslie exclaimed. "Will you play outside with us, Mama?"

"Can we build a snowman?" Daniel wanted to know. "There's enough snow for a snowman, isn't there?"

"We should be able to build a snowman," Renae conceded with a laugh, predicting a cold, wet mess on the kitchen floor later. She didn't care. The kids would have a great time frolicking in the snow, which meant she would have fun, as well. She hadn't quite outgrown her own delight in the rare sight of the clean, glittering white blanket draped over the outdoors, and the falling snowflakes dancing in the air.

Stirring oatmeal, Lucy said, "We'll have hot cocoa later. And maybe I'll make snow cream. I used to make that for your daddy when we had enough snow. He loved it. It's like homemade ice cream made with snow."

The twins grinned at each other in shared anticipation of winter fun.

Renae's phone rang again and she murmured an apology at this second interruption. "Good morning, Evan," she answered.

Lucy clattered her spoon against the pot of oatmeal she was scooping into bowls.

Hearing Evan's name, Daniel spoke urgently. "Tell him to come build a snowman with us. Okay, Mom, please?"

"I'll take this in another room," she said, avoiding Lucy's frown. "I'll be right back," she promised.

"Judging by Daniel's request, I take it you aren't going to work today?" Evan asked as soon as she let him know she was free to talk.

"No, Ann called and suggested I stay home with the kids. I took her up on the offer."

"That's why I was calling, actually. I was going to offer to come drive you to work. My truck is better on snow than your little car would be."

She was touched. "Thanks, but I'm not planning to leave home today. We have all we need to cocoon for a couple days."

"Good. Then I don't have to worry about you being on the highway with the morons that always come out in bad weather."

She laughed softly. "No. What about you? Are you going to your office today?"

"No, Tate and I told everyone to stay home. There's not much anyone can do in this weather. So if Daniel needs assistance with that snowman, I'm available."

She hesitated, thinking of how disappointed Lucy would be if Renae brought Evan into their day at home. Yet the children would be thrilled to have him there. She sensed that Evan was hoping she would invite him, maybe thinking a day romping with the twins in the snow would be fun for all of them.

As for herself—she was cowardly wishing she could go back to bed and hide beneath the covers rather than risk disappointing any of them.

"Renae?"

Knowing Evan was waiting for an answer, she cleared her throat. "I'd hate for you to get out on these roads."

"If you don't want me to come, just say so."

She was so focused on trying to keep everyone else happy that she was wasn't sure what she wanted even factored into the debate. "It's just that Lucy was planning to make hot chocolate and snow cream for the kids—"

"And she wouldn't want me anywhere near her at the same time," he finished grimly.

"Evan—"

She heard him draw a sharp breath before speaking evenly. "You know, I told you once that I wouldn't ask you to choose between me and Lucy because I knew I would lose. I thought I could be content with what you had left over to give, but you know what? Not so much."

Clutching the phone so tightly her knuckles ached, she groped for something to say.

He didn't give her a chance. "I've tried to be understanding about Lucy's pain. She's suffered too many losses in her life. But to carry this grudge against me for so long, so that you can't even mention my name or have me over to visit with your kids—well, that's hard to swallow. Regardless of any unwanted attraction I might have had for you in the past, Jason was my friend, damn it."

Unwanted attraction. Even though she agreed with the sentiment, the phrasing still stung a little. "I'll try talking to her again."

"By saying what this time?"

"The same thing I once said to you," she answered

flatly. "Jason made his own choices. Just because that last ride was your idea, it doesn't mean you made him go."

"Just the opposite, actually," Evan muttered.

She frowned. "What do you mean?"

After a slight hesitation that indicated he regretted the comment, Evan said, "Never mind."

"Evan—"

"I know your family is waiting for you," he said somewhat curtly. "Go make a snowman with your kids and drink hot cocoa with your mother-in-law. And sometime during this day, maybe you can think about whether you're satisfied with a Wednesday-night affair with me, or whether you want to figure out a way to have a hell of a lot more."

He hadn't given her an ultimatum exactly, she thought after he abruptly cut off the call. He'd simply made it clear that he was growing dissatisfied with their current arrangement.

Why couldn't Evan be like most men and be content with a no-strings affair? Instead, he wanted to make snowmen with her children and drink cocoa in her kitchen.

And what had he meant by implying that the motorcycle ride hadn't been his idea? Was there more to the story than she had heard?

"Well?" Lucy asked grumpily from the doorway. "Are you going to have breakfast or are you going to let this oatmeal harden to concrete?"

"I'm coming."

Lucy glared at the phone in Renae's hand. "Is he coming over? Because if he is, I can go over to Daisy and Maxine's for the afternoon, I guess. Just hope I don't fall in the snow on my way over."

Still clutching the phone, Renae planted her fists on her hips. "You would really leave if Evan comes over?"

"If he comes, I assume you would all be just as happy if I'm not here," Lucy replied with an affecting little catch.

"That's ridiculous. The children and I are never happier when you're not here."

Lucy's lip quivered. "I saw how their faces lit up when you said who was on the phone. I told you they would get too attached to him if you kept bringing him around. If he's here, they wouldn't even notice that I'm gone."

"Lucy, this is not a competition."

"Fine. If you'd rather have him here than me, I won't stand in your way."

Renae studied her mother-in-law in sudden realization. "You're trying to make me choose between him and you."

Lucy twisted the hem of her baggy sweater between her hands. "I'm not trying to make you do anything, Renae. You make your own choices."

"Yes. I do. Or I should. Instead, I've been driving myself crazy trying to do what everyone else wants me to do, to be what everyone else needs me to be. But maybe it's time I figure out what I want."

And the first thing she wanted, she realized abruptly, was to know what Evan had meant by that cryptic remark he'd muttered.

"I have to go out for a little while," she said, moving toward the doorway to fetch a coat and gloves. "I won't be long."

"You're going out? In this snow? Renae, that's crazy."

"I've driven on snow before. I'll be fine."

"But—"

"Tell the kids I'll be back in about an hour and a half to make that snowman with them. They can play video games until I get back."

"This is insane. You're going to crash your car."

"I'll be back in an hour and a half," she repeated. "Tell the kids."

Lucy was still protesting when Renae left the room.

Chapter Twelve

It took her forty minutes to make the usually ten-minute drive from her house to Evan's apartment. It would have taken even longer had it not been a little later than rush hour, and had she been driving in the other direction. Traffic in the westbound lanes into the city seemed to be at a standstill; she could only hope it had cleared some by the time she returned from this impulsive and probably ill-advised outing.

It occurred to her only when she parked in his snow-covered lot that she hoped he hadn't left his apartment since he'd called her. She was relieved to see his truck in its usual parking spot.

The snow was falling harder when she climbed out of her car. She'd neglected to bring a hat, so she turned up her coat collar and huddled into it as she trudged across the lot, her boots sinking into the untouched snow. Some children from the apartment complex played in the usually green compound behind the apartments and ripped up and down the now-buried walkway that ran along the river. Adult supervisors followed more sedately behind or brushed snow off the benches along the river walk to sit and watch. Renae heard the children squealing and laughing as they threw sloppy snowballs and inexpertly gathered snow for snowmen.

Her face felt half-frozen, her hair was damp and her teeth were chattering from both cold and nerves when Evan opened his door to her with a scowl. "What the hell are you doing here? You drove in this? After we talked about how dangerous it was?"

She shivered. "We need to talk."

He drew her inside. She'd stomped most of the snow off her boots downstairs, but she was afraid she was tracking in moisture anyway. Evan didn't seem to care. He disappeared for a few moments to return with a large bath towel that he draped over her when she stripped off her coat and gloves.

"You're cold," he fretted. "Come over by the fire."

Drying her hair, she made an impatient gesture with her free hand. "I'll be out in the snow with the kids later anyway."

"I hope you'll bundle up somewhat better than this when you do. At least wear a hat."

She tossed the towel aside. "What did you mean by what you said on the phone earlier? When I said the motorcycle ride was your idea, you said it was just the opposite. What did you mean by that?"

His jaw twitched. "Damn it, Renae."

She caught his arm when he would have turned away. "What did you mean? The ride *was* your idea, wasn't it?"

He hesitated, then nodded shortly. "Yeah, it was. You probably remember that I was in the state on leave visiting my grandparents in Batesville, at loose ends for the weekend. I thought Jason needed a day out to ride through the Ozarks, enjoy the fall colors. You know, before the babies were born. He'd seemed a little... well..."

Stressed, she filled in silently. *Anxious. Caged.* All emotions she had sensed in Jason in those weeks before his death.

He'd grown increasingly tense as the due date neared for the babies neither of them had planned on so early in their marriage. Just beginning his doctoral studies in addition to teaching high school, Jason complained about doing nothing but work and study and then having to help around the house. Renae, in turn, had pointed out acerbically that she was also working and doing most of the daily housework while carrying twins.

"Anyway," Evan continued, "when I found out he'd promised to help you that weekend, I tried to convince him that we could always go riding some other time. I even offered to help with the nursery instead."

His admission jolted her. She hadn't known about that offer.

"I'm sure I know what Jason said to you," she said through a tight throat. "The same thing he said to me. He wouldn't have many more free weekends to go out and have fun, and he didn't want to waste a chance."

"Something like that, yeah."

"You should have told me this before," she murmured.

He gave a slight shrug. "There was no need."

She sighed. "I know this hasn't been easy for you,

Evan. It must have been so hard for you to be there when Jason died."

She saw the haunted look in his eyes when he said, "That's an understatement. I had nightmares for a long time."

It was the first she'd heard of the nightmares. How self-centered had she been to be so focused on her own loss, and Lucy's, that she hadn't even realized the full extent of Evan's suffering?

She thought back to the funeral. Her heart ached when she remembered the way she had parted from Evan. Lucy had burst into tears when Evan had approached them at the simple graveside service, stark misery on his face.

"If you hadn't talked him into going out on that motorcycle you encouraged him to buy, my son would still be alive today," Lucy had accused him around her sobs. "I always hated those machines, but he had to have one to keep up with you."

His face pale, Evan had looked at Renae, as though trying to determine if she agreed with Lucy.

Her own heart broken, Renae had wrapped an arm around Lucy's shoulders, and turned to lead her away. She'd often wondered if Evan had taken her actions as a sign that she, too, had blamed him for Jason's death. Maybe she had, at least at that moment. Maybe, in her grief and regret, she, like Lucy, had simply needed someone to blame—and Evan had been a handy target.

He could have told her then that he'd tried to cancel the ride. But he'd seen no reason to do so. Perhaps because he'd understood their need to lash out. Or maybe because he had, perhaps unfairly, accepted some of the blame.

"I'm so sorry," she whispered. "After everything you'd been through, for Lucy to blame you... That had to have been devastating for you."

Though he shrugged, she saw the tightness in his face when he replied, "Like I said, I understood. And I still do, but I've got to say I'm tired of having to pay for the sins she thinks I committed."

"And I haven't made it any easier for you."

A spark of irritation flashed in his eyes. "No," he admitted. "You haven't."

She almost winced, but she knew he was simply agreeing with her. "I'm sorry. I guess I had some issues of my own to work through."

"You didn't trust me. You shared some of your mother-in-law's recrimination toward me. And you didn't think I would be interested in your daily life with your kids, so you thought I'd disappear once you started including me."

She frowned in bewilderment.

His mouth twitched. "You think I don't know how you think by now?"

She twisted her thawing fingers in front of her. "You have to admit my life isn't exactly exciting. I mean, between an office manager job and two first graders and a dog and a live-in mother-in-law, I'm always taking care of someone."

"You might not have noticed, but I'm hardly a party animal myself," he said wryly. "And I happen to think you have a pretty good life."

"So do I," she admitted, "but—"

"Not all men find the idea of marriage and kids repetitive and restrictive," he said gently.

At first she was too startled by his use of the word

marriage to understand the significance of what he'd said. And then it struck her. "You heard me talking to Kim when we had dinner?"

"Unintentionally." He ran a hand slowly up her arm. "Jason was very young, Renae. He'd have realized how lucky he was once the kids arrived and he got to spend time with them."

Maybe he'd put a few clues together, or maybe Jason had said some things back then. She nodded. "I'm sure he would have. It's just that we weren't getting along in the months before he died. That was hard for me to live with afterward."

This was the discussion she and Evan had been avoiding all these weeks. It was as difficult as she had expected—and yet, she felt a weight sliding slowly from her shoulders.

"He loved you, Renae. And I know you loved him. But he wouldn't have expected you never to love anyone again. That's not what he would have wanted."

"I know," she whispered, her gaze locking with Evan's.

Without taking his eyes from her, Evan rested his hands on her shoulders. "He would have wanted you to be with someone who appreciates all you've accomplished in the past seven years. Someone who admires your courage and your competence, your compassion, your commitment. Someone who loves you beyond all reason, even after he did his best to keep himself from falling for you."

Her throat was so tight now she could hardly breathe, much less speak. She blinked rapidly against a threatening film of tears, finally managing to force out a few words. "Yes. I think he would have wanted that."

He brushed a kiss against the top of her head. "Then I think he would have approved of us."

Her heart pounded against her ribs. Was he really saying—

"I love you, Renae."

Her knees went weak. She managed to straighten them before she collapsed, though she steadied herself with her hands on his chest. "You do?"

"I do."

Oh, wow. Something about the way he said those two words…

He continued to look at her, obviously waiting for her to say something.

"I love you, too," she said, her voice husky. "Why else would I have risked my life driving through a blizzard to get to you?"

He chuckled in response to the exaggeration, even as he covered her mouth with his.

The kiss was filled with so much emotion that she could feel her heart weep and rejoice all at once. Wrapped in his arms, she felt heat seeping back into her, filling deep, hidden places that had been cold and empty for a very long time.

She had loved Jason with all the intensity and drama of youth, with a gaping longing for a home and family of her own, someone to love and to love her in return. She had few regrets. She'd been fortunate to know him, and had been left with two amazing children and a wonderful mother-in-law because of him.

She loved Evan with the maturity of a woman who'd had the security and responsibility of a home and family for almost a decade, who had learned that life did not come with guarantees and that happy endings required a great deal of work and commitment to maintain. There were obstacles ahead but they would work together to overcome them. She looked forward to the challenges, even as she acknowledged how daunting they would seem at times.

Evan's hand slid down her back, tracing the dips and curves, cupping her bottom and pulling her closer. She felt his arousal and ached with her own, knowing the shivers that rippled through her now had nothing to do with the snow.

Snow.

She broke off the kiss with a low moan. "I have to get home. The kids—"

What might have been a sigh of regret escaped him, but he squared his shoulders and stepped back. "I'm driving you. There's another good inch of snow on the ground since you arrived. Don't worry—I won't come in, but I don't want you risking your neck in your car when I've got a four-wheel-drive truck."

"You'd better bring snow gear," she informed him. "Daniel's expecting you to help him build a snowman. And you know how he is—he's going to want a big one. Dinosaur-sized."

Evan hesitated. "What about Lucy?"

"Lucy is going to have to accept that you're a part of my life now, just as she is," she said firmly. "She tried to make me choose between you, but I refuse to make that choice. There's room in my heart for both of you."

His mouth twisted in a grimace. "It's not going to be easy."

"I think you're the one who pointed out once that nothing between us has ever been easy," she reminded him with a slight laugh, reaching for her coat. "We'll make it work."

Heading to his closet to get his gear, he smiled over his shoulder. "I believe we will."

A snowball hit Evan square in the middle of his back. Turning in the trampled snow to teasingly confront Daniel, he found Renae grinning at him instead, while her children giggled in delight.

"You're going to pay for that," he warned her.

She grinned. "We'll see about that."

Her face was red with cold, surrounded by strands of damp blond hair that had escaped the striped knit cap pulled down over her ears. A striped scarf wound thickly around her neck, and her puffy coat and gloves were covered with clumps of snow, as were her jeans from knees down and her waterproof boots. She looked silly, disheveled—and so appealing his blood heated despite the cold.

Dressed in their warmest clothing, the twins romped around them, throwing snow, wrestling with their hyperactive dog. A funny-looking snowman watched them play, his stick arms outstretched, his pebble smile beaming approval. The sounds of other children enjoying the snow drifted from other homes on the street.

Evan heard a distant siren and figured there'd been a fender bender nearby, ruining someone's snow day. Thinking about Renae jumping into her car to go to him earlier still made his stomach lurch. It had been challenging enough driving her back home in his four-by-four truck. Still, despite his exasperation with the risk she had taken, he couldn't help but be glad she'd come to him, he thought, smiling as he watched her playing with the twins.

As if they'd sensed him watching them, the trio turned en masse and rushed toward him with gloved hands full of cold snow. Laughing, he tried to ward them off, but they surrounded him, aiming for any small patch of exposed skin. Feeling a trickle of snow slide down the back of his neck, he growled and caught a twin in each arm, lifting them off their feet kicking and squealing.

"After I toss these two in the nearest snowbank, I'm coming back for you," he warned Renae.

Standing only inches in front of him, she hefted a snowball meaningfully. "You think so, do you?"

He simply couldn't resist brushing a quick kiss over her smile, savoring the feel of her cold lips beneath his.

"Oooh, Evan kissed Mama," Leslie crooned.

"Yuck," Daniel proclaimed, though he, too, seemed rather pleased.

Something made Evan glance toward the house. Lucy stood framed in the kitchen window, looking out at them. She turned and disappeared before he could see her expression.

He sighed and set the kids on their feet. So it wasn't all going to be laughter and kisses. He still didn't regret the commitment he had made to this family.

"We'd better go in now," Renae said a few minutes later, igniting a chorus of protest from the kids.

"You're cold and wet," she told them with a firm shake of her head. "You can play in the snow again later, but for now you need to go inside and get warm."

They stopped on the back stoop to stomp and brush off as much snow as possible. Renae had left a stack of towels just inside the kitchen, and they all made use of them as they stripped out of wet outer gear. Lucy was nowhere in sight, though a big pot of homemade chicken noodle soup sat on the stove, the burner turned low to keep it warm, and a covered pan of corn bread was on the counter.

Making sure they were both dry, Renae sent the kids to wash up for lunch. "It's almost an hour after they usually eat," she confided to Evan when the kids ran from the room. "I'm sure they've worked up an appetite."

Sniffing the air appreciatively, Evan nodded. "They aren't the only ones."

Renae chuckled. "If that's a hint, it isn't necessary. Of course you're welcome to—"

He looked around at her when her voice trailed off. "What's wrong?"

She was staring down at a sheet of paper in her hand, her expression a mixture of frustration and distress. She looked up at him with eyes suddenly luminous with tears. "Why does she have to be so damned dramatic about everything?"

It wasn't necessary for her to identify the "she" in question. Evan sighed. "What does it say?"

"Lucy's moving out," she said dully. "She said she has come to the realization that her grief and fear of being alone has caused her to hold me back from having my own life."

Her breath caught. "She hopes we'll be very happy and that we'll let her see the children sometimes," she added irritably. "Can you believe that?"

Hearing the pain behind Renae's aggravation, he came to a decision. "Where is she?"

Renae folded the note and stuffed it in a high cabinet,

presumably to keep the children from finding it. Maybe so she wouldn't have to see it again herself.

"She's gone next door to our neighbors' house. She said she'll stay in their guest bedroom until she finds a place of her own."

Evan reached for his coat.

Renae pushed a hand through her hat-mussed hair. "Where are you going?"

"To bring her home," he said, shrugging into the still-cold garment.

"Evan, maybe you should—"

He was already headed for the door. "Save me some soup."

His left hand in his pocket, he stood on the porch next door a few minutes later, pushing the doorbell. Snow had started to fall again, more lightly now but steadily. Children still played in yards up and down the street and a variety of snow people and animals were in various stages of construction. Evan ignored the cheery winter wonderland, focusing instead on the door in front of him.

A white-haired woman in a rather garishly colored sweater and red stretch pants opened the door to him. "Yes?"

"I'm Evan Daugherty. I'm here to see Lucy Sanchez." He figured she'd heard his name before, though he wasn't sure he wanted to know in what context.

"I'm Maxine Whelan, Lucy's friend." The woman eyed him appraisingly through her glasses. "I don't know if she'll want to see you. She's a bit upset."

"Would you mind asking her?" He thought of adding that he was prepared to stand outside in the cold until

Lucy agreed, but somehow that didn't seem like a very effective threat. Lucy was just as likely to let him freeze.

Lucy appeared behind her hostess. "I'll see him, Maxine."

"You're sure?"

"Might as well get it over with," Lucy said grimly.

Maxine and her sister Daisy left Lucy and Evan alone in a doily-and-knickknack-cluttered living room. Lucy sat on the couch, leaving Evan to perch uncomfortably on an undersized chair.

"Why are you here, Evan?" she challenged.

He gave her the same answer he'd used with Renae. "I came to bring you home."

"That isn't my home. It's Renae's and her children's. I've just been living there with them."

Though there was a stubborn set to her expression, she was obviously threatened by the changes occurring in her family, uncertain of her place. He needed to convince her that while change was inevitable, it did not always lead to upheaval.

"As I understand it, you've been a major part of making a home for them. Renae says she wouldn't have been able to get by if it hadn't been for you."

"I'll still help her out when she needs me," Lucy conceded. "But it's time for me to find another place to live so Renae can have a life of her own."

"You've decided this because of me," he said bluntly.

She twisted her fingers in her plump lap. "Well, yes, mostly. Renae should feel free to bring her, um, friends to her home for dinner. She and the children enjoy spending time with you, and since you and I are uncomfortable together, that makes it difficult for them. And if you and she... If Renae decides she would like to remarry in the future, it's obvious I would have to move out anyway. I might as well go ahead and do so now."

"Okay, let's address that latter part first. Why, exactly, would you have to move out if Renae remarries? She enjoys having you in her home…the kids benefit from living under the same roof with a loving extended family—why do you think anyone would want to change what is working so well?"

She shot him a narrowed, openly suspicious look. "You're saying if you, for example, were to marry Renae, you'd want me to live in the same house with you?"

"I fully intend to marry Renae, though I haven't asked her yet," he answered evenly, surprisingly calm considering he had just made that decision. "And it never occurred to me that you weren't a part of the package. You are her mother, in every way that counts. Her children's grandmother. They adore you. Maybe we could find a slightly larger house, but I can't imagine that you wouldn't be welcome in Renae's home. I've promised her I will never ask her to choose between us, and I'll keep that promise."

Lucy seemed struck by much of what he'd said, but one sentence apparently stuck out to her. "You want to marry her?"

Maybe he should have mentioned that little detail to Renae first, but he answered honestly, "Yes."

"Do you understand what you're getting into? Her children will always come first with her. You'll be expected to be a—" she stumbled, but continued doggedly "—a father to them. Your presence will be expected at school programs, sports meets, dance and piano recitals. You'll be there when they're sick. There will be tantrums and emergencies and fights, first dates and traumatic breakups, the expense of braces and clothing and college. Are you prepared for that?"

He swallowed, understandably nervous at the litany of responsibilities he would be taking on. "As prepared as I can be."

"You'll never be prepared for growing to love them and then losing them," she whispered. "Whether it's because they grow up and move away or…or something else…."

"No," he admitted, pushing a hand through his hair. "I can't imagine being prepared for that."

They both sighed.

"As for whether you and I can be comfortable together," Evan continued, "that's something we can work on for the sake of the family."

She looked down at her hands, trying to hide the tears that had started to leak from her eyes.

This must be the day for opening old wounds, he figured. But maybe that was the only way they were ever going to heal.

"I know you blame me for Jason's death, Mrs. Sanchez," he said brusquely. "I could argue that he made his own decisions and that it was only fate that let me get through that intersection ahead of him. I could tell you that I loved my friend, and that I would have given anything to trade places with him that day. But none of that would bring him back."

Still looking down, she sniffled and wiped at her face with one hand. His heart twisting in response to her misery, Evan pulled out the handkerchief his Southern mother had trained him to carry. "It's clean," he said, offering it to her.

Without meeting his eyes, she accepted the handkerchief and dried her cheeks, though moisture continued to leak from the corners of her eyes. "Renae said that seeing you, for me, is a painful reminder that Jason is no longer here."

"I'm sure she's right."

"Yes. But she doesn't blame you. She said the only person we should blame is Sam Abbott."

"No. She doesn't blame me." Not anymore, anyway. "But she wasn't Jason's mother," he added gently. "I can't fault you for having resentments against me, Mrs. Sanchez. I just hope we can find a way to make peace now."

Lucy drew an unsteady breath. "I suppose we can try."

It was a tenuous truce, at best, but he would take what he could get. "Then come home, will you? The kids want to show you their snowman before Boomer knocks it down, and I've got a bowl of pretty delicious-looking soup waiting for me. I'd like to eat it before it gets cold."

At the mention of the word *home,* she rose, though she still looked at him with a measure of misgiving. He figured it would be a while before he proved that she could trust him. With her daughter-in-law, with her grandchildren—and with her own future security.

"If we're going to live together eventually, I guess you might as well call me Lucy," she told him rather grudgingly.

He chuckled wryly. "Thank you."

They turned together toward the doorway only to find themselves face-to-face with Renae, watching them both with tear-filled eyes.

Lucy gave a little gasp of surprise. "Where are the children?"

Renae straightened and swiped quickly at her face with the back of one hand. "Maxine and Daisy are with them. They sent me here, in case either of you needed backup. But you both seem to have been holding your own."

"How long have you been standing there?" Evan asked with a slight wince.

She met his eyes with a smile that made his heart pound. "Long enough to know to expect a proposal."

"And do you have an answer ready?" he asked huskily.

Her smile turned to a shaky laugh. Though the answer was in her eyes, she shook her head. "You'll have to ask me before you find out. And as much as I love my mother-in-law, I'd just as soon we do that in private."

"I'll get my coat," Lucy said, moving toward Renae. She patted Renae's arm on the way past, a gesture that looked to Evan like a mixture of affection and apology.

Evan moved toward Renae, sliding a hand down the arm of her coat. "You could have let me know you were there."

"I didn't want to interrupt. Besides, I owed you an eavesdropping."

He had to acknowledge the truth of that. "Maybe we should agree that neither of us will eavesdrop on the other in the future."

She nodded. "I can agree to that."

With some satisfaction, he took that as another acknowledgment that there would be a future between them.

Cupping a hand behind her head, he kissed her lingeringly, not really caring if Lucy or Daisy or Maxine or the whole darned neighborhood saw them.

Finally breaking off the kiss, he smiled down at her. "Let's go home."

Entwining her fingers with his, she turned toward the door with him. "I like the sound of that."

* * * * *

REQUEST YOUR FREE BOOKS!
2 FREE NOVELS PLUS 2 FREE GIFTS!

SPECIAL EDITION
Life, Love & Family

YES! Please send me 2 FREE Harlequin® Special Edition novels and my 2 FREE gifts (gifts are worth about $10). After receiving them, if I don't wish to receive any more books, I can return the shipping statement marked "cancel." If I don't cancel, I will receive 6 brand-new novels every month and be billed just $4.49 per book in the U.S. or $5.24 per book in Canada. That's a saving of at least 14% off the cover price! It's quite a bargain! Shipping and handling is just 50¢ per book in the U.S. and 75¢ per book in Canada.* I understand that accepting the 2 free books and gifts places me under no obligation to buy anything. I can always return a shipment and cancel at any time. Even if I never buy another book, the two free books and gifts are mine to keep forever.

235/335 HDN FEGF

Name   (PLEASE PRINT)

Address   Apt. #

City   State/Prov.   Zip/Postal Code

Signature (if under 18, a parent or guardian must sign)

Mail to the **Reader Service:**
IN U.S.A.: P.O. Box 1867, Buffalo, NY 14240-1867
IN CANADA: P.O. Box 609, Fort Erie, Ontario L2A 5X3

Not valid for current subscribers to Harlequin Special Edition books.

Want to try two free books from another line?
Call 1-800-873-8635 or visit www.ReaderService.com.

* Terms and prices subject to change without notice. Prices do not include applicable taxes. Sales tax applicable in N.Y. Canadian residents will be charged applicable taxes. Offer not valid in Quebec. This offer is limited to one order per household. All orders subject to credit approval. Credit or debit balances in a customer's account(s) may be offset by any other outstanding balance owed by or to the customer. Please allow 4 to 6 weeks for delivery. Offer available while quantities last.

Your Privacy—The Reader Service is committed to protecting your privacy. Our Privacy Policy is available online at www.ReaderService.com or upon request from the Reader Service.

We make a portion of our mailing list available to reputable third parties that offer products we may interest you. If you prefer that we not exchange your name with third parties, or if you wish to clarify or modify your communication preferences, please visit us at www.ReaderService.com/consumerschoice or write to us at Reader Service Preference Service, P.O. Box 9062, Buffalo, NY 14269. Include your complete name and address.

HSE11B

SPECIAL EDITION

Life, Love and Family

NEW YORK TIMES BESTSELLING AUTHOR

KATHLEEN EAGLE

brings readers a story of a cowboy's return home

Ethan Wolf Track is a true cowboy—rugged,
wild and commitment-free. He's returned home to
South Dakota to rebuild his life, and he'll start by
competing in Mustang Sally's Wild Horse Training
Competition.... But TV reporter Bella Primeaux
is on the hunt for a different kind of prize,
and she'll do whatever it takes
to uncover the truth.

THE PRODIGAL COWBOY

Available September 2012 wherever books are sold!

"What I actually said was that this doesn't make sense."

She cocked her head, frowning. "This?"

His eyes once again met hers. And held on tight.

Oh. This. Got it.

Except…she didn't.

Then he reached over to palm her jaw, making her breath catch and her heart trip an instant before he kissed her. Kissed her good. And hard. But good. Oh, so good, his tongue teasing hers in a way that made everything snap into focus and melt at the same time— Then he backed away, hand still on jaw, eyes still boring into hers. Tortured, what-the-heck-am-I-doing eyes. "If things had gone like I planned, this would've been where I dropped you off, said something about, yeah, I had a nice time, too, I'll call you, and driven away with no intention whatsoever of calling you—"

"With or without the kiss?"

"That kiss? Without."

O-kaay. "Noted. Except…you wouldn't do that."

His brow knotted. "Do what?"

"Tell me you'll call if you're not gonna. Because that is not how you roll, Patrick Shaughnessy."

He let go to let his head drop back against the headrest, emitting a short, rough laugh. "You're going to be the death of me."

"Not intentionally," she said, and he laughed again. But it was such a sad laugh tears sprang to April's eyes.

"No, tonight did not go as planned," he said. "In any way, shape, form or fashion. But weirdly enough in some ways it went better." Another humorless laugh. "Or would have, if you'd been a normal woman."

"As in, whiny and pouty."

"As in, not somebody who'd still be sitting here after what happened. Who would've been out of this truck before I'd even put it in Park. But here you are…" In the dim light, she saw his eyes glisten a moment before he turned, slamming his hand against the steering wheel.

"I don't want this, April! Don't want…you inside my head, seeing how messy it is in there! Don't want…"

He stopped, breathing hard, and April could practically hear him think, *Don't want my heart broken again.*

***

Look for
THE DOCTOR'S DO-OVER
by Karen Templeton
this September 2012 from Harlequin® Special Edition®.

HSEEXP0912